THE COLLECTOR PAPERBACK

VI CARTER

CONTENTS

WARNING

WARNING

This book is a dark romance. This book contains scenes that may be triggering to some readers and should be read by those only 18+ or older.

ALSO BY

Other Books by VI CARTER

THE CELLS OF KALASHOV
THE COLLECTOR #1
THE SIXTH #2
THE HANDLER #3
THE BOSS #4

MURPHY'S MAFIA MADE MEN
SINNER'S VOW #1
SAVAGE MARRIAGE #2
SCANDALOUS PLEDGE #3

SONS OF THE MAFIA
SINS OF THE MAFIA #0.5

YOUNG IRISH REBELS SERIES
MAFIA PRINCE #1
MAFIA KING #2
MAFIA GAMES #3

MAFIA BOSS #4

<u>WILD IRISH SERIES</u>
FATHER (PREQUEL)
VICIOUS #1
RECKLESS #2
RUTHLESS #3
FEARLESS #4
HEARTLESS #5

<u>THE BOYNE CLUB</u>
DARK #1
DARKER # 2
DARKEST #3
PITCH BLACK #4

<u>THE OBSESSED DUET</u>
A DEADLY OBSESSION #1
A CRUEL CONFESSION #2

<u>BROKEN PEOPLE DUET</u>
BREAK ME #1
SAVE ME #2

CHAPTER ONE

NICHOLAI

STROBE LIGHTS BOUNCE OFF every space, and the flow of the dancers is broken from one motion to another. Bodies pulse and sweat out their sin. The playground of sin: Gail's. The club has built up a reputation for just that.

I move two kissing women aside, their faces blissfully staring up at me as I move past them. All around me reminds me why I love Gail's. I come here when I need to forget who I am and what I do. But tonight, I'm not here for pleasure. I'm working.

Pavel is my next target, the one I must collect and deliver to the can. I always get twenty-four hours from the moment I receive the message to have them placed in the can to be collected by someone else. I never wait around; it's not my job to know what happens after I deliver them.

A woman who appears possessed jerks and falls to the ground. The crowd moves back but continues their dance around her. I glance around until I find who I seek. Dimitri. I nod and he moves away from the wall and clears a path toward me.

"A woman has collapsed." I jut my chin behind me.

"Thank you, Nicholai." Dimitri vanishes into the crowd. His body is clad in black leather, covering up all the tats that I know are painted onto his body.

He once worked within the Bratva, but somehow he found a way out. I have no idea how many lives it cost for him to leave, but I'm sure he gave up someone he shouldn't have in order to get out. Working with him is frowned upon, but he moves close to the circles I moves in, so making an enemy of a man like Dimitri isn't wise.

I break through the crowd and climb the five steps that are cushioned with red carpet. The chain that stops the clubbers from crossing is removed for me before I even have to pause in my stride.

"Pavel?" I ask.

"Third room on your left."

I nod as the chain is placed back onto the hook. I take in a lungful of cleaner air. It's tinged with a different kind of sin, but one I'm accustomed to. The heavy hitters take up most of this part of the club. I reach the third door and pause. I take out my gun and make sure it's loaded before stuffing the piece back into the band of my trousers. I glance left and right, then knock three times. The door opens slightly.

A bellboy is ready to dismiss me, but his eyes slowly widen. I place my finger over my lips before beckoning him forward with two fingers. He hesitates and I tilt my head, then he wisely steps out of the room and races past me.

"Who's at the door?" Pavel asks.

I step into the darkened room and gently close the door behind me. It takes my eyes a moment to adjust to the lighting in the room. Pavel is seated with his back to me. A girl dances in a glass box. She's naked, her head thrown back as she runs her hand down her body and in between her legs.

I look away from the blonde beauty and walk to Pavel.

"I asked who's there!" His irritation has him ready to turn.

I grip his chair, freezing it in place. "Enjoy the show a few more minutes, Pavel."

He tries to turn, but I grip his shoulders, forcing him to stay put.

"The Collector."

I'm not sure if my title is said with fear or a plea, maybe both, but either way, I hold Pavel still and watch the blonde touch herself. Her other hand runs up to her large breasts, where she grips her nipples and squeezes.

"I can pay." Pavel's lame attempt at trying to bargain has me dragging his fat ass out of the chair.

"Time to go." I push him toward the door.

He stumbles before spinning around. His face grows gray as he runs a fat hand through his thinning dyed-black hair. "I can pay."

I crack my tattooed knuckles. "You know who I am?"

He nods. "The Collector."

I'm easy to identify, and I like that. It gives the person around thirty seconds to come to terms with the knowledge that I'm here to collect, and I always collect. My hair is tied up, both sides shaved. A black cross is tattooed into the side of my head—it's one of my markings, my identifier for who I am. Pavel's gaze tightens.

"Have you ever heard of anyone not being collected?" I ask while taking a step toward him.

He shakes his head.

"Let's go."

He turns toward the door and opens it, knowing his fate is sealed. The chain is removed for us as I keep my gun pressed into Pavel's back. I didn't want him to get brave and try something stupid. He weaves through the crowd, and I nod at Dimitri as I leave.

The moment we're outside, Pavel starts to plead again. "Name your price."

I remove the gun from his back and tuck it into the band of my trousers. Pavel glances at me over his shoulder with hope in his eyes, like I might have changed my mind. I reach out and grip the back of his neck, directing him to my car that's parked down the next alleyway.

"Please, I can give you anything you desire."

"I don't desire anything," I answer him, as I keep a check around us, making sure no one is watching at this hour of the night. The streets are devoid of much life. In the next thirty minutes, they will bustle with the clubbers, as the doors to Gail's will close.

My car bleeps, the orange lights flashing in the dark alleyway. I wave my hand close to the trunk and it opens. Pavel tries to talk, but I push him in and slam the trunk down on him. His thumps start, but the moment I get in and the engine purrs to life, the music drowns out the beating of his fists.

I drive through the city and out into a more barren landscape. Out here in the wilderness is an outhouse, or what we call *the can*. It's where I leave each person I collect, and from there, at some point, they are picked up by someone and brought to Victor. I have no idea what happens to the people. All I know is that each time I deliver someone new, the can is empty, its previous occupant gone.

Each person I collect has done a wrong that has gotten the atten-tion of Victor. So, that's never good. I turn off onto a dirt road. I'm aware of the dust that dances and no doubt sticks to the sides of my black Audi I just had cleaned.

The sun breaks across the sky, painting it in oranges and reds. I pull the car over and get out. Pavel isn't banging anymore. I pop the trunk and he blinks a few times.

"Get out."

He climbs out. "Who sent you?"

I slam the trunk and jut my chin out toward the small building. "Walk."

Pavel does.

"Victor sent me." I've never met Victor, but he's my boss and you don't disappoint him.

"Why?" He tries to glance at me over his shoulder, and I push him on. "I don't know. All I know is who I have to collect."

I open the lock on the door and stand back for Pavel to enter. He leans in but doesn't enter the concrete box. I push him in and he spins. "Please, I will give you anything."

I close the door and lock it. His fists collide with the steel door. Every person I place in the can does the same, like it might make me turn around and set them free. I climb into the car, and the engine roars to life. If I let them go, my life would be taken instead. I slap on a pair of sunglasses and drive back to the city.

The large black structure catches the rays of the sun, making all the angles of my home sharper. The gates open and I drive slowly up the winding driveway until I pull into the garage. My phone dings in the dock, and I remove the device before getting out of the car. Entering the house through the kitchen, I turn on the coffee pot and pull my tie off from around my neck.

I open the message, which was sent from an unknown number.

Mila Ivanov. Detain within the next twenty-four hours and keep her until further notice.

I reread the message twice. This is new. I've never kept someone I had collected before. An uneasy feeling skitters up my spine, but I'll do my job. I always do.

CHAPTER TWO

MILA

"**G**OOD MORNING, IGOR." I hide a grin as he tries to tackle the weeds that have overtaken the flower bed.

"It is not a good morning, Mila." He stands with hands on his hips and looks down at the mess. My brown satchel hits my hipbone, and I push it toward my back.

"I think you should remove it all and not even bother trying to separate the weeds from the plants." It's too hard to tell which is which.

"I think you're right, Mila," Igor says. Soft blue eyes smile up at me. He's been a resident of this apartment complex since before I moved in six years ago. He's been a constant in my life, helping to balance out my unpredictable past, which I've buried. When I moved in here, it was a new start for me.

"I better get to work." I touch his back gently, and Igor waves me off as he tackles the overgrown mess. I live close to Teapots, which is where I waitress.

I pull my satchel back to the front, and it hits my bum as I walk. I glance over my shoulder, tugging my wine-colored coat tighter around me. I have the sense I'm being watched.

I'm naturally a paranoid person, but I don't think anyone could blame me, if they knew my past. I quicken my steps and continue to peek over my shoulder, but each time I look behind me, I'm met with mocking emptiness. Strong hands grip my arms, and I swing around, nearly walking into a man.

"Oh, sorry," I say as I glance down at the tattooed hands and all the way up to a pair of dark eyes. Something deep inside me stirs and runs in fear. His hair is tied back, the sides shaved. The black cross tattooed onto his head has me stepping out of his large hands. He towers over me, and I lock my knees to keep upright.

He nods before stepping around me. I can't breathe as I turn and watch his large frame clad in a dark suit walk down the sidewalk. He never looks back, but my throat grows taut. I know who he is. My vision wavers and I stumble forward. My mind won't settle as I automatically arrive at work. Removing my bag and jacket, I wrap an apron around my small waist.

The Collector.

I just met The Collector. He had to be here for me. *But he's gone,* I try to tell my racing heart. *He's gone. You are fine. You're here at work.*

I grab my pad and pen and give my boss a tight smile as I make my way out onto the floor. I'm unsteady and my mind is frazzled. Was he here for me?

Of course he came for you, Mila. You knew he would.

I scold myself as I step up to a table and take the order from the couple. I scribble it down and walk away, giving the order to the cook. I start to clear off tables. I need to run. I need to go right now! What am I doing?

I fill a tray with dirty plates and try to tell myself that maybe he had someone else to collect. Fear clutches my throat, and I press my palms onto the table like I might be able to stop the onslaught of emotions that threatens to pour out of me.

I straighten and walk over to my boss.

"I'm so sorry, Elena. I need to go."

"You just got here." She frowns. "Are you sick? You do look pale."

"She always looks pale." Kat laughs from the kitchen, and I force a smile that doesn't last.

"Yeah, I'm not feeling well at all."

Elena nods. She's a good boss, and I'm a good waitress.

"Thanks, Elena." As I get my bag and coat, I try not to glance around the space. I might never see it again. I can't stop the tears that burn my eyes, but I refuse to let them spill. I leave out the side door. I don't get far before I press my back against the stone wall and take in gulps of air.

I want to scream. Running isn't an option, but I got six years. I know I only got those six years because of Victor. I wasn't hidden here. It was an illusion that he'd sold to me, and I bought it without question.

I push off the wall and start the walk back to my apartment. I'm waiting for The Collector to appear and grab me, but no one does.

Igor's gray eyebrows rise, and I try to force a smile for him.

"Forgot something." I wave him off and his eyes narrow slightly, but he goes back to his job. I take out the keys to my apartment as I climb the steps.

I keep thinking of running, but I already know how silly the idea truly is. Yet, the survival part of me won't give in.

I open the door, and the smell of my vanilla candle is the first thing to greet me. My stomach tightens and I meet my blue eyes in the mirror. I drop my gaze as I pull off my jacket and hang it up. I close the door and enter the kitchen, which is already a small room. Now it shrinks to nothing as The Collector sits at my table with his tattooed hands joined. My gaze jumps to the spiderweb tattooed on his neck. He did time in prison. Being Bratva made his list of possible crimes long.

I untie the apron I forgot to take off. My stomach tightens as the chair screeches along the floor as The Collector rises.

"You've come to collect," I say without meeting his gaze. I fold the apron with the same care I always give it.

Biting on the inside of my jaw stops the onslaught of tears that want to spill. I want to ask to take a final walk around my home. Maybe take some photos I kept from my childhood. I know I'll never return.

What I might be going back to has me hunching my shoulders. Death looks like a better option, but I'm a coward. I never could end things; I didn't have it in me. It would have been kinder to myself.

"Pack a few things," he clips.

I frown at him. I didn't expect that courtesy, but I would take it. Pack a few things, like what? Pictures, clothes, toiletries? Would I be returning to the mill? My stomach coils.

You made it through it once, you can do it again.

But could I? Tears spill and I wipe them away fast as I randomly grab clothes and toiletries. I finally grab the photo album before unplugging everything in each room. The Collector waits in the kitchen. His arrogance nearly makes me want to run, but I know he can kill if he wants.

My mouth waters and I swallow the saliva. I return to the kitchen with my bag and The Collector rises. His eyes don't meet mine. "Let's go."

I pull the bag up on my shoulder and take one final look at my small kitchen. Some part of me that knows what's coming shuts down, and I become numb as I follow The Collector to his car.

He pauses when he reaches it and opens the trunk. I sling my bag in and walk to the front of the car, where I open the passenger door. I glance up to see The Collector staring at me. He closes the trunk before walking to the driver's side. His eyes don't release me until he disappears inside the car. I get in and focus on fastening my seat belt—the tremble in my hands has me attempting to lock the belt three times before I succeed.

I watch the wall move past me in a blur. Liddi's screams send waves down my spine, and I try to curl my body in on itself. I can't go back there. Panic claws up my throat and I silence it.

One, two, three, four, five... I count until I lose count and have to keep starting again. I count as tears stream down my face and my body is racked with trembles I can no longer control. It's like my nerves are crackling and popping, and I can't stop the assault on my body.

The slick car under me barely allows the rough surface to affect its occupants. My stomach churns. Blood money, that's what paid for a car like this.

I glance at The Collector. His neck is coated with tattoos. There are more skulls and crosses tangling themselves in the web. A thick scar is woven with a gray snake. Being this close, I can see the ragged skin, otherwise it looks like two snakes intertwining.

The car slows and we pull up to the black marble structure. The gates slowly open, and with each inch they part, I can sense my doom.

CHAPTER THREE

NICHOLAI

T HEY NORMALLY FIGHT, SPIT, and scream. They beg me and offer me everything and anything. I glance at Mila as I pull into the garage. Already so much about this situation is different. She hasn't stopped this process once. Women are normally worse than men. I don't get many, but when I do, they cry and dig their heels in. I've even had sexual offers made in exchange for their freedom. The second odd thing about Mila is that she is the first person I didn't have to bring to the can. She's also the first person in my home.

Blue eyes heavy with despair glance at me. I open the car door and yank off my tie. "Get out."

She does without hesitation. She's also the first person I've collected who rode up front. I pop the trunk and get out her bag. When I look up at her, she's staring at her feet. I close the trunk and enter the house, and she follows. Now this is the part I'm unsure of. Steam rises from the full coffee pot. After throwing her bag and my tie onto the counter, I get myself a cup. She's standing in the doorway, her eyes drawn to her bag.

She's beautiful in such a natural way. She isn't like the women I usually find attractive, but I can still appreciate her natural beauty.

Her breasts are small, maybe a handful—I normally like them big and artificial. She crosses her arms over her chest like she knows my thoughts. I take another sip from my coffee and observe her from over the rim. What am I to do with her? I could get a message at any stage to drop her to the can. Maybe they hadn't picked up Pavel yet and they didn't want two of them together? The thoughts of Pavel near Mila turns the coffee sour on my tongue, and I put it down.

"Do I have to give you a list of rules, or do you understand you're mine for now?" My gaze roams over her, and she pushes her shoulders back, but she can't stop the fear that pools in her eyes or the tremble of her lip.

"I understand."

I nod and open the top two buttons of my black shirt. "Good."

I leave the kitchen and check my phone as I climb the glass steps. My designer said they gave the illusion of more space. I hadn't disagreed, but each time I look down, my stomach flips slightly. I'm not afraid of heights, but I'm not a fan of them either.

My suit jacket drops on my bed before I pull off the shirt. Mirrors coat every wall in my room. I like the illusion, especially when entertaining. No one can hide.

Each mirror reflects my tattoo-covered torso—I have no more space left for ink. Earlier, Mila's eyes took in the ink on my neck, and her eyes widened, like she had a notion of what they meant.

I push down my trousers and boxers, then enter my bathroom, which is a complete wet room. Pulling the tie out of my hair, I step in under the spray, and my cock grows hard as I think of the blonde who had danced in her glass box for Pavel. She couldn't see who watched her; it was a one-way mirror. All she would see was herself doing very naughty things. The bleep of my phone has me knocking off the water, my cock still begging to be touched as I pick up my phone.

Another collection. This is a first. Three so close together.

Dimitri Smirnov. Detain within the next twenty-four hours and take to the collection point.

My hard cock dies quickly as I drop the phone onto the bed. This is why I have no friends. I don't have anyone who I care about, because all it takes one message, and if I have to deliver them, I will.

I take out another black suit. I know where Dimitri will be tonight, so his capture will be simple. After getting dressed, I retie my hair before going back downstairs. Mila is still in the kitchen, standing right where I left her.

Throwing my cold coffee down the sink, I turn to Mila. I can't just leave her here. I need to tie her up. I rummage through the drawer, then withdraw a roll of heavy black duct tape. When my gaze meets hers, her eyes widen and she takes a step away from me.

The house is new, so some of the rooms haven't been finished yet. I pull a chair from the table and leave the kitchen.

"Come on," I tell Mila and carry the chair and duct tape to the first empty room. The walls have been painted, and blinds cover the windows. I drop the chair and draw the blinds. Mila hovers in the doorway, her eyes scanning the room.

"Sit down on the chair." I open the duct tape and she hesitates, but eventually, she walks over to the chair and sits down. I've never had someone do exactly what I say. Normally, they lash out, try to run, but Mila sits down and focuses on her hands. I want to ask why Victor wants her. I want to know what she did to get herself in such a situation. But it's a rule of mine—I don't ask questions.

After tearing off a lump of duct tape, I cover her mouth, and she whimpers but doesn't pull away as I continue to tie her to the chair. The duct tape circles her small waist, and for extra measure, I tie her legs to the chair. When I stand back, I'm satisfied that she won't be going anywhere.

I turn off the light and pull the door closed behind me. I turn the key, then pocket it before making my way to Gail's.

"Nicholai, what can I do for you?" Gail, the owner of the club, greets me. The tight green wraparound dress sits perfectly on her toned body. She's in her early forties—she says late twenties, but she keeps herself well. Her short hair is spiked, and she wears an open and friendly smile. She's ruthless behind it all.

"Has Dimitri started his shift?"

Gail glances at the Rolex on her slim wrist. "He's late. He's never late."

Fuck.

He knew they would send me after him.

"Pavel was a good customer of mine. He spent a lot of money here."

"If you want him back, talk to Victor."

Gail nods, but that snippet of information serves her purpose for this conversation. What is she searching for?

"Victor?" She raises one arched eyebrow.

"It's not a secret, Gail. But right now, I'm starting to feel like you're wasting my time." I brush past her but start to run when I hear her curse. I remove the gun from the band of my trousers and point it at the sliver of light that appears and then disappears as Dimitri escapes out the exit door.

"You'll be hearing from me," I shout over my shoulder at Gail before I leave through the door Dimitri left through.

"Stop running!" I shout after him and I aim my gun. I can take a shot if I want to. I'm allowed to wound, and if it's the only way to bring them in, I can kill. I lower the gun as he disappears around the corner and out of sight.

CHAPTER FOUR

MILA

I'M BREATHING STEADILY THROUGH my nose, but each time I think of it, I'm sobbing into the duct tape before I calm myself down. The fear is growing, and I need to control it. I'm exhausted as tears soak my face. The walls around me start to close in, and no matter what I do, I can't stop the memories pouring in. I scream into the tape and push all my weight to the left before swinging to the right. The chair tilts but lands back correctly, and it's all I need. I keep rocking until I finally get what I want. I land on the ground hard, my head taking the brunt of the fall. Pain explodes behind my eyelids as warm liquid pools beneath me, and for the first time, I welcome the loss of time. I welcome the sanctuary the darkness offers me.

The room is tinged with red. Wasn't it white before? I blow out a painful breath through my nose, and the pool of blood ripples as the air races across it.

I groan and try to roll, but the pull on my body has me groaning again. I wiggle my legs and pain explodes in my head. The creak from the leg of the chair has me keeping my eyes closed as the leg of the chair breaks free, freeing my leg.

I'd laugh... only the pain increases behind my eyes. I wasn't even trying to escape. A laugh bubbles against the duct tape. My cheek is cold. The liquid is alarming, but I close my eyes and try to find the darkness again.

I crane my neck back as the door opens. His polished shoes move toward me, and I look up at him. Dark eyes that have seen too much blink once and then twice. He steps away from me and peels off his suit jacket, then he folds it and lays it on the floor. His tie is next. Fear jackhammers in my throat as I try to raise my head from the floor. Bile claws up my throat, and I have no choice but to swallow. He unbuttons the sleeves of his shirt as he assesses me. What is he going to do?

He cracks his knuckles and walks toward me. My body buzzes with shivers, waiting for the blow that will finish me, but nothing happens. Opening my eyes, I'm faced with an empty room. A sob pushes against the tape on my mouth.

He arrives back in with a basin of water. I close my eyes as he straightens the chair. I'm ready to spew everywhere but force it down.

He leans over me and separates my hair without a word. He's gentle as he cleans my head with a cloth. I recoil from his touch, and he holds me still with one hand pressed firmly on my shoulder. The basin of water soon turns red and he gives up.

The knife in his hand could be a blessing. Is he going to make it quick? Did Victor order him to keep me here and kill me? I know this isn't the job of The Collector. He doesn't take people home.

The duct tape falls away from my waist and legs.

"You broke my chair." It's the first time he's spoken since arriving back in the room. Dark eyes, which hold nothing, focus on my face. His long fingers clutch the duct tape. "This is going to hurt." He gives me the warning before tearing the tape off my face, along with a layer of skin.

I wince in pain. The burn continues long after the duct tape is gone. I lick my lips. They feel raw.

"Can you stand?"

I force myself out of the chair, and the world tilts sideways. I'm falling, but strong arms and the smell of cologne wrap around me. I turn my head away from his chest as my stomach finally rebels, and I empty the contents onto the floor. Once my stomach settles, he exhales loudly and carries me from the room. I keep my head away from him as he carries me upstairs. It's like we're walking on air. I blink and my stomach shifts again. The steps are made of glass. Who has glass steps? I squeeze my eyes shut.

"Don't sleep."

His warning has me opening my eyes, but I realize the worst that could happen has already happened. They've found me. I close my eyes and don't open them again until my back meets cushions.

I'm in a double bed, the sheets a deep gray under my hand. A door to a bathroom is open, and The Collector returns with a washcloth. Blood stains the end of his rolled-up sleeve. I roll my head so I face the window as his huge frame makes the bed dip, and he starts cleaning my head again. Now, hitting my head didn't seem very wise; the ache is growing. But at that moment, I wanted the memories to stop.

His hand parts my hair gently, and a part of me wants to see his face. It's a dangerous part of me that has recognized how gorgeous he is. The devil always wears the mask of an angel. The Collector works for Bratva bosses who are ruthless. He is no better than them.

He gets up with no explanation. His footsteps are light for such a huge guy. I squeeze my eyes shut and try to focus.

I know the rules. I know how this works. So why am I here in The Collector's house? Based on the fact that things are different, I need to try to escape. I don't have to be a sitting duck, but no one outruns The Collector. Yet, I never heard of The Collector taking his jobs home. Does he know who I am? Does he know what Victor did to me?

I swallow more saliva and keep my eyes tightly closed as he reenters the room.

"Don't fall asleep."

His warning has me opening my eyes and glancing at him. A dangerous shiver rattles my bones, and the idea of escape breaks apart, turning into a mist that dissolves completely.

He sits back down, and my gaze roams over the tattoos that coat both his arms, his fingers, his neck, and as far as his shirt will allow me to see. There isn't a blank space on his tanned skin.

"Face the window." His accent is a mingle of Russian toned down to something Irish.

I want to ask him about it, but I turn away. Getting friendly with The Collector isn't wise. Not that he would answer my questions anyway. My thoughts cease as a sharp needle enters my flesh. My stomach heaves with the tug on my head. I try not to picture a needle and thread in his hands.

I open my eyes and focus on the sky—clouds move past and reshape, but I can't make a picture out of them like I could when I was a kid. Spending hours lying in the lush green grass with my brother was how I'd pass the time. I squeeze my eyes tightly as a final sharp pain erupts at the back of my neck. I automatically go to rub it.

"Don't touch it."

My hand falls back to my stomach, and The Collector stands up.

"Don't sleep for a few hours." The tips of his fingers are coated in blood, and his eyes hold no warmth as he steps into the bathroom.

The sound of running water has me sitting up. The ache in my head has me slightly worried. What if I have an internal bleed? I'm itching to touch my neck, but I keep my hands resting on my stomach.

The Collector leaves the bathroom, and when his heavy eyes land on me, I sink deeper into the bed. The room shrinks quickly, and I'm tempted to close my eyes. He dries his hands on a small navy towel as he stares at me. When he's finished, he doesn't speak but leaves the room. The key turns in the door, and I'm not sure if I want to sink into the bed now that he has gone or cry because I'm alone, once again, with my thoughts.

CHAPTER FIVE

NICHOLAI

OPENING THE WINDOWS AFTER cleaning up the vomit, I'm ready for this mission to end. I'm aware of the time that is passing. I have twenty-four hours to get Dimitri. Glancing at my phone tells me I have sixteen hours left. I open my tracking app and have a sense of satisfaction when Mila's red dot blinks to life in the upstairs bedroom. She hasn't moved off the bed. After I stitched her head, I placed a tracking device into her neck. It's the only way I could leave her alone and make sure she stayed where I left her.

I shower and change into a fresh black suit, then leave the house again.

The neighborhood I pull up in has too many unemployed people loitering on their porches. All eyes swing to my Audi. Drugs, poverty, and violence have taken away any form of civilization from these people. I could understand how Dimitri wanted to live amongst them. It reminded him of the Bratva. It was a unit, a law upon itself. It was belonging. No one sits on his porch. I hadn't exactly expected a welcoming committee. After checking both guns, I place one in the holster around my ankle, and the other I stick in the band of my trousers as I exit the car.

The shift in the air is so brief; it's like the rattle before the crack of thunder. These people recognize me and slowly they make their way into their homes. Locks are turned and soon the street is devoid of life. I move along the white panelling of Dimitri's home as I make my way around back. The back door is unlocked. I pause for a heartbeat and remove the gun from my waistband. He knew I would come; he isn't stupid. I lower the gun and step into a tidy kitchen. My gaze bounces across the washed-down counters before jumping to Dimitri, who stands in the doorway that leads to the hall.

"You could always say you didn't find me."

I grin. I don't put my gun away but lower it to the ground. "I find everyone."

Dimitri doesn't return my smile. "I have a daughter." His admission adds a layer to him I don't want to see.

"You can come with me without a struggle, or I can drag you to Victor."

His laugh fills the small kitchen. "Have you ever met Victor?"

His question has me raising my gun. I don't do this. I don't talk and debate. Debating means there's room for a negotiation, and there isn't.

I don't want to shoot him, and he is unarmed. Placing the gun in the band of my trousers, I clear the space between us.

"Move," I order.

His lips curl up. "You don't have to do this." He raises both hands like I have a choice.

"Move." I give the final order and curse him as he pulls a knife from his sleeve. I lean back as the silver dagger swipes the air. It's a kill shot—he tried to cut my throat. He swings quickly, not giving me much time to recover. I met his arm with my own. The knife vibrates in his fingers before he loses his hold and it sails across the room. His eyes widen but flicker toward the back door. The creak of the hinges has me diving to the ground. I remove both guns and point them at my targets. The guy pauses in the door, and he hasn't a chance. I pull both triggers, and two bodies hit the ground.

I get off the ground and holster my guns before wiping down my suit. The guy who's face down at the back door bleeds out on the tiled floor. I kick him onto his back. He looks like one of the porch occupants. Maybe a friend of Dimitri's. I check his pocket for a wallet but find none. I'm ready to dismiss him as a neighbor when a tattoo behind his ear catches my attention. A small picture of an octopus.

I grab him by the arms and drag him away from the back door, then get into my car and reverse it up the driveway and pop the trunk. After rolling out some plastic, I grab two gallons of petrol and take them inside the small house. Dimitri is heavy, but I carry him out and place him on the plastic in the truck of my car. The wound between his eyes leaks, and I wrap the plastic around him before returning to the house. I douse each room in petrol and lead a trail out to the driveway, then drop a match and watch the line of petrol burn as it makes its way into Dimitri's house.

I pull out and see curtains shift as I drive through the small neighborhood. Dimitri's house blazes behind me, but no one comes out of their homes to investigate.

I leave Dimitri's body in the can and drive back to Gail's. She's there when I arrive, and I see the disappointment at seeing me.

"You tried to have me killed by one of your goons."

She stands tall and wraps one hand around the other that hangs in front of her. "I have no idea what you're talking about."

I smile at her as I move closer. "No worries, he's dead. Both of them are."

It's there, in the depths of her dark eyes. She had a thing with Dimitri.

"I didn't think you would get attached to someone. You know, in this game, we all have to be lone wolves."

Her laughter is forced. "He kept my bed warm. That was it."

I move closer so I'm towering over her. "If that's all it was, why did you send one of your men to kill me?"

It's the first time I see the indecision in her eyes. "I didn't send him to kill you. I only sent him to warn Dimitri."

I don't believe a word she's saying. She's lying through her pearly whites.

"You inconvenienced me."

Gail holds my stare before raising her hand and clicking her fingers. A young boy comes forward.

"Nicholai would like to be entertained. Give him whatever he wants."

I grin at Gail. "I'll take the offer, but it doesn't erase what you did." I leave the threat hanging and follow the boy to the back rooms.

"What would you like, Mr. Nicholai?"

I want a blonde with big boobs, but only a small blonde with blue eyes and small breasts fills my mind.

"Brunette," I say as I sit down in the chair. The lights dim and the boy leaves. The box lights up and I wait. I'm kept waiting for a brunette wearing a white thong and nothing else to step into the box. Her gaze meets mine, but I know she can't see me. She's meeting her own eyes in the mirror. She smiles before a slow beat fills the space and she starts to move.

I exhale and command my body to relax as the brunette turns around and bends down, showing me her ass. Her hands run across her cheeks before she slaps them hard, and my cock twitches. She turns and runs her hands across her chest. I press the button and the glass box rises into the air. She's startled for a moment, but she descends the steps and walks over to me.

I rise and push my boxers and trousers down before sitting back down on the chair. The brunette smiles at me before she falls to her knees and takes my cock into her mouth. I let my head fall back as her warm mouth encircles my cock. She rides it up and down with her mouth. When she removes herself and replaces her lips with her hands, I don't like it.

"Suck it," I say.

Her warm breath rushes across my cock before she takes in as much as she can. It's not deep enough. Grabbing her hair, I help her move up and down. I need this release, especially after a kill. Dimitri's dead body flashes in my mind, and I push the brunette's head down on my cock and pull her up quickly; the pleasure has me moving her faster.

My balls ache for release. The sac's full and coated in the girl's saliva as I keep her head moving fast up and down on my cock. She gags, but I want more; I want my release. I grab her face with both hands and fuck her mouth hard. I pound into her and can feel the release build up until I jerk into her mouth. Three more slams empties me, and I release her.

She coughs but swallows and wipes her mouth. She doesn't speak but stands and walks back to the box. Once she's inside, I press the button and the glass moves back down. She looks startled as she leaves the box through the door, and I pull up my trousers expecting to feel satisfied, but I don't.

CHAPTER SIX

MILA

MY HEAD STILL ACHES, but I'm very aware I've been left alone and I'm not tied up. I try the door, but it's locked. Going into the bathroom, I meet pale blue eyes in the mirror.

Blood is caked along the side of my face and down my neck. My blonde hair is stuck to my head in a tangle of blood and knots. If I'm to escape, I need to clean myself up without attracting attention. I don't linger in the shower but wait until the water runs clear. My hands run along a lump on the back of my neck. I must have hit it when I fell. My fingers feel for stitches, but there are none. I can examine myself better when I get out of here. I dry quickly and place my clothes back on my damp body.

From the sideboard, I remove the candle from its marble perch and use the holder to smash the door handle. It takes a few tries, and the noise level has my heart hammering, but I get the door open and leave.

Downstairs, I open all the drawers until I find some loose notes. It's only a few hundred, but it's a start. I open The Collector's fridge and take out a few slices of cheese and stuff one into my mouth before leaving the house. I have no idea how much time I have left, but I need to get out of here. The wall isn't high, and I glance around for cameras but don't see any. I easily climb across the low wall and land softly on the other side. I'm on the street and try to keep my walk to a stroll so I'll appear like someone just out walking.

I never would have dreamed of running from The Collector. There's still that voice that tells me this is pointless and silly, but it's like the rules have changed. I'm in his home and if the rules change, it means I have a chance. I might be able to hide and start again.

My skin feels cold, and I wrap my arms around my waist. There's still blood on my white top, but pulling my hair to the side keeps it covered up. I keep walking for another twenty minutes, grateful I don't come across a car.

My heart pounds and my feet eat up the road as I race after the bus that's ready to pull out. My fist hits the side.

"Wait." Panic tears through me. This is my chance. The bus stops. The hiss of the door opening has me grabbing the bar and meeting the eyes of the angry driver. I climb up the three steps and hand him a twenty.

"I'm sorry." *Please don't kick me off.*

I glance at all the annoyed gazes that focus on me. I pull my hair across my top as the driver hands me my change and ticket. I'm not even seated when he takes off, and I fall into a seat and shift over to the window as I watch the small town disappear.

Excitement has me smiling at the girl in the window. She smiles back, but a flash of red along her white top has me pulling my hair over it.

Imagine if I'm the first person who ever escaped The Collector. I'm giddy at the idea, but reality comes crashing back and I sober up.

I doze off several times as the light slips away and night darkens the interior of the bus. I'm back in a steel bed. It's been such a long time since I've been here, and the fear vibrates down to my soul. I suddenly sit up, and the driver hovers over me. I tighten my hands around my waist.

"This is the final stop."

My heart races and I manage a nod. He moves back so I can walk through the empty bus. Getting off, I look up and down. A closed gas station seems to be the only place here.

"Is there a motel close by?" I ask.

He frowns. "It's four miles that way."

I nod.

"A girl shouldn't be out here alone."

I force a smile at his concern, get off the bus, and start to walk toward the hotel. Ghosts walk beside me, and I try not to hear their words, their cries, their taunts.

The mill was filled each night with screams of pain, screams of pleasure, and something in between. We called it the pit. It was the center of hell to most of us. No one came back. Well, I was the exception to that rule. I was starting to see a pattern forming, especially with The Collector. I only got out of the mill because Victor had said so. I shiver again and wrap my arms around my waist.

I want the world to scatter away from me. I don't want to feel the cold breeze or the ghosts who walk around me. I want someone to take me from the dark I had been dropped back into.

Is that where The Collector will finally take me? To the mill? What a cruel fate. It seems exactly like something Victor would do. I've walked for a while, my mind consumed with my painful past, but I manage to smile through it all.

The pink neon motel lights flash ahead. I hasten my pace as I walk across the empty lot and to the front desk. A female glances up at me from behind the desk. I try not to look so broken and tired and force another smile.

"I'm looking for a room, please."

She glances behind me. "Just one?"

My pulse spikes and I slowly turn, expecting to see The Collector behind me with his dark, soulless eyes, but the space is empty.

I frown. "Yeah, just one."

I slide a fifty across and get back a ten along with the key. The number twenty-two is carved into it. I take the key and stuff the change back into my pocket. Outside, the world is asleep. I have no idea what time it is as I push the key into the door.

The smell has me covering my mouth. It's a mixture of urine and fags. I close the door behind me and hold in the cry that wants to spill from my lips. Opening the window does no good. I enter the bathroom and flush the toilet, but the smell of urine is strong from the bedroom.

The towels are fresh, and my exhausted body wants me to lie on the bed. I draw the curtains and lock the door before going back into the bathroom. I take all the towels with me and cover the bath before I get in. I keep one, a hand towel, and push it against my mouth so I can scream.

I've been running my whole life, and I think of ending all this pain and anger, but I'm not strong enough. My screams turn to sobs before they turn to angry shouts. My feet slam against the side of the bath as I continue to let the pain flow from my soul. Liddi's scream join mine, and bile crawls up my throat. I'm out of the bath and empty the cheese I ate into the toilet.

A knock at the door has me reeling and I stand up. My legs are unsteady as the knock sounds at the door again. My tears dry up as I hold the wall and make my way to the wooden door. The doorframe leaves my fingertips as the knock sounds heavier this time. He's found me. There was nowhere to go, nowhere to hide.

"Hello," a female voice sings, and I push off the wall, recognizing the voice of the receptionist. Relief has me opening the door, and she holds a stack of towels.

"You forgot these."

I take them. "Thank you, but there were some here already."

"Maybe the last person didn't use them." She's lingering and I go back into the room.

"Thanks," I say.

Her gaze flickers to the left. "No problem." She leaves and I'm ready to close the door.

A shiny black shoe lodges itself in the doorway. I stumble back, the towels scattering out along the floor as The Collector enters the room. He closes the door behind him.

"Running is never an option." His words hold nothing. Like I am nothing.

I'm sick of meaning nothing to people. I want to be big like them. I want to crush their souls, strip them bare and see how they feel.

I stumble back further as he steps deeper into the room.

"Running is my only option." My heart races when he pauses. "You'd run too if you knew where you would end up."

He holds up a hand. "You did a wrong, so there is a price to pay." The words that leave his mouth have my fear evaporating into the air.

"A wrong?" I grit my teeth as my nose burns with angry tears. "The only wrong that I and thousands of other women seem to have done is to be born."

His dismissive eyes have me taking a step toward him.

"Born into the hands of horrible and immoral human beings just like you." My words whip out, but he doesn't flinch. "Move."

He steps aside so I can start to walk.

My shoulders drop forward, and a sob I can't keep in falls. "Please," I beg and for the first time I see some kind of emotion in his dark eyes. "I haven't done anything wrong."

I join my hands together, wondering if the devil will allow me to step out of this room with my tattered soul.

He takes a looming step toward me. "You all say that." He curls his nose up, and I'm not sure if it's me or the smell of the room.

I lash out and he grips my hands easily. Fear shoots through me and rattles my bones.

"You shouldn't have run."

His large hands still grip mine, and I'm shrinking at his sheer size and power. I need to give up this idea that should have never formed in my head. The idea that I could outrun this.

"If there is a grain of kindness in you, you would end this for me." I grip his hands back, and he releases me, his brows drawn down.

"If you want out that bad, why not do it yourself?"

The question has angry tears burning my eyes, and I half sob and half laugh. "Because I'm a coward." Who stayed curled in a corner as Liddi screamed for me. I was her home, yet when she needed me, I sank to the ground and screamed along with her.

"Move."

I blink. Tears spill and I unsteadily leave the motel room.

CHAPTER SEVEN

NICHOLAI

I WAS RAISED BY my mother. My father died on the streets when I was six. My mother warned me away from the life that claimed her husband and three brothers. She pleaded with me, but I wanted to be feared. To me, it was a rich ingredient that was designed for real men.

I'm walking behind Mila. Fear has her body trembling, and I've never felt like less of a man. If my mother were alive, she would be disgusted.

I climb into the car and Mila gets into the passenger seat. Her hands tremble as she clips in the seat belt.

"If you don't want to live, why did you run?" I don't ask questions—it's a rule. Yet here I am again, breaking it.

"Obviously I want to live." Fire in her blue eyes has me starting the engine and leaving the motel. "How did you find me?"

She sounds unsure, like her question is silly. But it isn't. She got away fast. I would have eventually found her without the tracker. She would have been picked up on CCTV or used her name at some stage. Everyone messes up eventually. Most people I'm sent after are where they're supposed to be.

"It was simple, really. The bus only goes to one place, so I checked each stop. The last stop had only a gas station, and when I came across the motel, the girl described you."

"Simple," she says shortly.

I can tell she's staring at me and glance at her. She huffs before glaring out the window. I tighten my hands on the steering wheel, not understanding at all why she's getting under my skin so much.

"How's your head?" I ask.

She sits up straighter. "You care?"

Do I? I push my foot down harder on the accelerator, wanting her out of my car. "You owe me a door," I say instead.

She laughs and digs into her pockets. Money rains down on my lap and I glare at her.

"There you go." Her chest rises and falls, and she looks like a woman that's been pushed to the brink. But I can't have her break with me. I didn't sign up for this shit.

She screams as I tug the steering wheel and jam on the brakes. The car behind us sits on the horn. Removing my seat belt, I turn to a terrified Mila. About fucking time.

"You stole from me."

Her nostrils flare as she scrambles for air.

"You damaged my property. You made me chase you."

She's shaking her head like I've said something that isn't right.

"Now, you think you can be smart with me."

She pulls in her bottom lip and sinks her teeth into the soft flesh.

"I didn't do anything wrong." She looks around the space. I don't think she's referring to the list I just delved out.

"He just wants me to suffer." She blinks and tears spill down her face.

I laugh. Since when did I become a babysitter? Her tears are getting to me, and I'm starting to feel soft.

"You pull one more stunt on me and you'll be sorry." I leave the empty threat in the air and start to drive. I'll do nothing. I've never laid a finger on a woman and I'm not about to start now.

I drive back to the house. She doesn't say another word and gets out. We go right back to the start, and she stands in the kitchen and waits for her orders. Tying her to a chair didn't work. Locking her in a room didn't work.

"Sit down." I point at the chair, and she takes a step back. I cut her a warning look, and she finally sits down on the chair.

She's small, like if you grabbed her she could crumble in your hands. I fight a grin as I open the fridge. I have no idea why she's turning me on so much. I'm staring into the fridge with no idea what to make. Taking out a cheese spread, I glance up to find her watching me. Her cheeks redden. After cutting up Vienna bread, I coat both sides with the cheese spread. She takes in each step I make before I place the plate in front of her.

She doesn't speak as she picks it up and starts to eat. I take a bite of mine before pulling off my tie and jacket. The cuffs of my shirt are stained with blood from Dimitri. Two shirts in one day. What are the odds? Ever since Mila stepped into my life, it's really gone to shit.

"How long were you in prison?" Her question is spoken softly, but it's like a bolt through my system.

"You think I'm going to answer your question?" I turn while rolling up my sleeves, and her eyes drink in all my ink.

"It's only a question." She shrugs before taking a bite of her sandwich.

"It's never only a question. You ask one, you ask two."

Her cheeks redden again, and I return to my own bread and take a bite.

"Well, if I ask you a question, you can ask me one."

What is she playing at? Who wants to have a conversation with The Collector? A desperate kind of person, that's who.

"There is nothing about you that I want to know."

She finally shuts up and finishes her food.

I head upstairs, and she follows me obediently.

We pass the room where she smashed the door in. I don't really care about the door. I'm impressed she tried to escape. I hadn't thought she would have tried, to be honest.

The room I take her into has a four-poster bed. She's gnawing on her lip again. Her legs lock, and I walk around the bed and open the top drawer to take out two pairs of handcuffs. I hold them up for her to see. I'm wondering if she'll run, but she doesn't. Her eyes dull as I walk around to her. She shrinks in size when I'm beside her.

"Get on the bed."

Her eyes move up to me before her lids quickly flutter closed. She sits on the edge of the bed and stares at the floor. I press one of the handcuffs around her wrist and make her move closer to the top, where I clip them into the hook I had placed at the head of the bed. It isn't for keeping people captive.

Her eyes widen when she sees the designated hook. I move around to the other side of the bed and take her other hand, making her lie back in the center. Her intake of breath is loud. She's seen the mirror overhead. I glance up and meet her wide eyes, surprised to see curiosity mixed with fear in them. The click of the second handcuff has me looking away from her.

I walk down to the end of the bed. She raises her head off the pillow. "What is this?"

"More questions. What do you think it is?" I ask and she lets her head fall back into the pillow, but not before I see the color in her cheeks.

"I'm not going to rape you."

Her head snaps up.

"I've never forced myself on a woman. I've never needed to." I leave the end of the bed. She's tempting. A taste of her would be nice, but I meant what I said. I wouldn't force myself on her.

CHAPTER EIGHT

MILA

HE LEAVES ME ALONE again. I listen as his car starts up, and I tug uselessly at the handcuffs like I might make an impact. It's hard not to meet my eyes in the overhead mirror, and I'm imagining what he must look like from that angle. My body burns with the thoughts he's provoking in me. I've never felt this level of attraction to a man. Maybe it's because he took me. Maybe the darkness of it is adding to his appeal.

I tried talking to him in the kitchen, but that was pointless. His eyes constantly told me he was undressing me. I'm not used to being around men, not since the mill.

I bite my lip. I could try to seduce him. I don't have any other options, and maybe it would be an offer he would take me up on.

He said he would never force himself on me, and some part of me believed him. I lie in wait for his return, but exhaustion has me falling asleep. I wake to a dead arm. I had lain on my arm all night. I pull and the chains rattle. I'm glancing around the room, wondering how long I've been asleep.

The door opens and The Collector steps in. The green V-neck jumper he wears is such a difference from the suits. My heart leaps for too many different reasons. He steps up to me, and I try to control my breathing as he unlocks my handcuffs.

"What time is it?" I ask.

Of course he doesn't answer. There's a watch on his wrist, which I try to read upside down. I'm sure it says seven in the morning.

"Go to the bathroom and tidy yourself up." He puts the handcuffs in the drawer as I roll off the bed.

My clothes are crumpled, and I'm sure I smell badly from the motel room. I enter the bathroom, and he doesn't follow. I close the door and quickly relieve myself. I wash my hands and face and am just turning off the tap when he steps into the bathroom. His ability to shrink spaces has the air stilling in my lungs.

Seduce him. The whisper is quick and I have to keep the laughter in. I'm sure I look great this morning. I've never seduced a man before; I didn't think that's what men wanted. But I take a step toward him, ready to try.

I swallow as he folds his large arms across his chest. He has the sleeves pushed up, showcasing all his ink. My heart dips and falls around my chest as I step up to him and crane my neck back.

"I can do things." I start to scold myself—I sound like a child saying, *Hey, I can do magic.* He doesn't blink, but some part of me recognizes the humor in his dark eyes.

"Things..." I blow out a breath, telling myself to walk away. But he doesn't move, and I take that as an encouraging step. "Things that men like." I'm speaking to his chest, really selling myself. Liddi's laughter has me taking a step back, and I blink.

"You couldn't please a man even if you tried." Her words taunt me, and I feel my cheeks burn.

"You're making me an offer I don't think I can refuse." The Collector's words hold laughter in them, but he isn't smiling.

"I'd rather die than touch you." My embarrassment turns to anger, and he unfolds his arms and takes a step closer to me.

"Is that so?" He doesn't sound happy. This was some seduction.

"It doesn't matter." I try to get out of the bathroom, and he blocks me. I glance up at The Collector.

"What things can you do?"

Is he taunting me? Making fun of me? I have no idea, but now is my chance. *Just say it and do it, and he might consider helping you.* The lies I tell myself.

"I can please you." I hold my head high. It's a small price to pay. All the girls at the mill had to do it. I could do it too.

Liddi always said to try to find some enjoyment in it.

"Please me." The Collector holds out his hands, and my stomach hollows.

He's serious. It's simple. All I have to do is wrap my mouth around him and suck up and down. That's what Liddi said. I push her face aside. I need to be something or someone else. Just for now, just for this moment.

"Anytime today would be nice."

I snap my gaze up at The Collector. His dark eyes dare me, and I move to my knees. I'm waiting for him to stop me, but he doesn't. I unbuckle his jeans and open the button. I'm waiting for him to laugh, but when I pull down his jeans, I can see his erection through his boxers. He looks huge—too huge for my mouth.

I feel more confident as I pull down his boxers and his large erection is there. All of it, in my face, and I don't know what to do, so I touch it with my hand. I know he's watching me, and my heart won't slow down. I'm ready to bolt, but I tell myself I can do this. I can make him come. I ignore the wetness between my legs as I continue to stroke his cock, trying not to wonder what it would feel like inside me.

His groan surprises me, and I stop and look up at him. His dark eyes swirl, and I feel even braver. I push my lips to the head of his cock, and it jumps in my hand. I lick it, loving its reaction to me. I kiss the head again before wrapping my mouth around it and taking as much of him as I can into my mouth. He fills me, and I let his cock back out.

Everything in me stirs to life, and I wonder if I might come without him even touching me. I push my lips down on his large cock again and he groans, so I move faster. I can't take him all in my mouth. Holding his shaft, I stroke him and my lips follow suit, leaving a trail of saliva my hand glides over. His moans have me moving faster, and I startle when warm seed flows into my mouth, which I swallow instinctively.

I release him and his head snaps down to me, so I touch him again and watch as his seed spills on the bathroom floor. He reaches down and pulls me up. My back collides with the wall as he towers over me. I'm not sure what he's doing, but my body sings as he touches me. There's a sense of foreboding, and I close my eyes as he pushes his palm against the outside of my pants. I'm a bundle of nerves, and I know it won't take much to make me come. He touches the band of my trousers and I react, slamming my palms into his chest. He stumbles back.

"Don't touch me."

Anger lights in his eyes. I don't want the blowjob to have been for nothing. I know I'm messing up, so I clear the space between us and press my lips against his. I don't know what he'll do, but when he lifts me and holds my body to his like I weigh nothing, I come to life with a need I've never felt.

I wrap my legs around him, feeling his cock grow hard against me again, and I have no idea what's happening. I'm losing control of this situation. His lips are soft and warm against mine. My mind drifts off to forbidden places like what he would feel like inside me. What it must be like to be handcuffed to the bed and see him above me. He breaks the kiss, and the heaviness in his eyes has my stomach squirming. He untangles me from him and reaches for the waistband of my trousers again, but I freeze under his touch. He pauses, sensing the change.

"I don't want you to touch me," I tell him.

He holds his hands up and steps away. I want to erase my words, but he doesn't seem angry this time. He pulls up his trousers and boxers.

"Come downstairs when you're ready for breakfast."

I nod. My cheeks burn again. I just gave The Collector a blowjob. I just gave my first blowjob.

I hope it was worth it.

CHAPTER NINE

NICHOLAI

MY BODY STILL HUMS with want for Mila. I flip the egg in the pan as she enters the kitchen. Her cheeks are still flushed. She pulls the white long sleeves over her hands, which she crosses against her chest. My gaze flickers to her swollen lips. Her lips were perfect around my cock. I turn back to the pan, and a chair creaks as she sits down.

The toast pops and I place it onto the plate along with her egg. I've never cooked for anyone but myself. I place the plate in front of her, her cheeks still aglow, making her look innocent, but I need to remember she has the attention of Victor. She isn't innocent in all this, no matter how pure she looked or how unsteady she was as she touched my cock like it was her first time.

"Thank you." She doesn't look at me as she picks up her knife and fork. I get my own plate and sit across from her.

She's gnawing on her swollen lips and my cock twitches. This is going to be a long day. The sound of the gate bell has Mila's head snapping up, and she glances at me. Fear widens her blue eyes.

I get up and go to the hall. A silver car is pulled up in front of the camera. The driver presses the button again, and I lift the phone.

"Hello."

"Nicholai. Open the gate." Oleg glares into the camera, and I push the button to open the gate.

"Who was it?" Mila asks the moment I step back into the kitchen. I don't like the idea of Oleg coming to my home. My stomach twists. He's here to collect her.

"Go upstairs to your room." I have no idea why I'm sending her up, but I don't want her touched.

"My room?" she stutters.

"Now!" I bark.

She pushes out her chair, and her small frame moves quickly past me. I keep an eye on her until she disappears up the stairs.

Oleg enters the house with arms wide. "Nicholai!"

I greet him with a hug. "Oleg, to what do I owe the honor?"

He touches my face before looking around the space. "I like what you have done here."

He takes a silver box from his jacket and removes a thick cigar. Two more men enter, crossing their arms in front of them. The last one closes the front door.

Cigar smoke fills the hallway as Oleg blows it around him.

"I'm here on personal business from Victor." Oleg inhales again as he walks into my kitchen, his two bodyguards moving along with him.

"It's not like Victor to send a personal messenger," I say, folding my arms across my chest.

Oleg laughs and coughs up puffs of smoke. "This is important."

I unfold my arms. There's a gun in the cupboard behind him. Two knives are under the table, and a shotgun lies behind the radiator. Two tiles are liftable, and under them are more guns. I still have one strapped to my ankle. I'm pinging the escape routes and how many guns these three men carry. So far, I've clocked five. The odds aren't good, but I've had worse.

"I'm here for Mila." He's watching me closely.

"Are you here to collect her?" I hate the sick feeling in my stomach.

"I'm not The Collector."

No, you're an errand boy who can't be touched.

I leave the kitchen and see her peek from the corner of the wall. She never went to her room. Her gaze clashes with mine, and for the first time, I want to apologize.

"Come down."

She moves along the steps, her hand running along the wall like it's the only thing keeping her up. When she reaches me, I grip her arm. I want to tell her to run, but she did something to bring this upon herself. I release her and she steps into the kitchen.

"Mila, Mila," Oleg greets her, and I don't return to the kitchen straight away, as I try to compose myself.

"Oleg." She says his name with a hitch in her voice. She knows him.

I enter the kitchen, and Oleg inhales his cigar before blowing smoke into Mila's face.

"I want a word with Mila in private." His gaze dances to mine.

"This way." I lead him to a sitting room.

"This will do." He looks around him.

I'm tempted to stop Mila again as she steps into the room. Her shoulders are hunched forward, causing frustration to claw at me. She's a job. I need to treat this like a job. I know I'll deliver her to the can, so this need to protect her... I have to get rid of it.

"You can leave." Oleg smiles up at me.

Mila keeps her back to me, and maybe that's for the best. I leave the room, and his two bodyguards step up to the door, blocking me from entering. I leave the sitting room and get my phone. I turn on the tracking app, and Mila's red light comes to life. She's standing still.

Her eggs and toast are going cold on the kitchen table. I can't stop staring at them. I leave out the back door and inhale a few deep breaths of air. This sense in me is building. I can't control it, the need to go in there and protect her. She gave me a blowjob. Is that why? I laugh at my own reasoning. Hundreds of women have given me blowjobs and I've never wanted to protect them.

I pace outside before moving to the front of the house. His car is unlocked, and I open the passenger door. I look up at the house, and nothing stirs close to the windows as I hunker down and look inside. Opening the glove compartment, I find a gun and two phones, but nothing else. I do a quick sweep of the car, but it's clean. After closing the door gently, I move back to the house.

When I enter the kitchen, Oleg is at the sink. "She's very comfortable here." He's speaking, but I'm focused on the blood on his fists. Every fiber of my being wants to demand whose blood it is, but I hold still.

"I want her tied up in that room until we return for her." He glances over his shoulder at me and shakes his hands out. Droplets of blood flick out onto my sink.

"She seems very comfortable here. Victor wouldn't like that." Blood rushes through me, and I control the violence that wants to be unleashed. "When will she be collected?"

Oleg turns off the tap and picks up my dishcloth to dry his hands with. "I'm not sure, but I won't be a stranger."

He smiles at me, and I've never wanted to kill someone so badly. The sense that tries to override the calm in me and everything else isn't normal.

He pats my shoulder but pauses. "I'll be in touch." I want to shrug his arm off my shoulder.

"I look forward to it." My mouth moves automatically, and I don't do anything as they leave my home. The car hums and rolls down the driveway. I walk to the front door and watch as the car leaves and the gates close slowly behind Oleg.

CHAPTER TEN

MILA

O LEG—HOW I HATE HIM. I move my legs, but my stomach screams as I try to make myself smaller. I open my eyes as the door closes and Oleg leaves me. My body aches, but I remind myself I'm alive. The pain is telling me I am very much alive.

I move my fingers in front of my face and none seem broken after he bent them back. I tighten my hand into a fist and close my eyes. I wish I was as strong as them. I wish I could fight back. My cheek aches from the slap he gave me.

"You're a dirty little whore." His slap was delivered with those words.

The door opens and I don't move off the floor. I'm not sure I can. The Collector fills the space, and his eyes grow dark. A look of savagery twists his handsome face. He covers his lips with a finger, telling me to be quiet.

I close my eyes. I don't want to speak to him; he has no power. Oleg waltzed in here and did whatever he wished. Me thinking that seducing The Collector would keep me safe was stupid and naïve. My eyelids flutter open as The Collector picks me up. I groan as pain racks my body. He lays me onto the couch and leaves the room. I fight the tears that threaten to fall.

I move my jaw left and right—it aches—but once again, I can confirm that nothing was broken. He punched me like I was a lump of meat. Anger claws at me, anger that I don't let go of as The Collector arrives back into the room. He kneels on the floor beside me. The click of handcuffs has me looking at him. He tightens one around my wrist; my other hand is left free.

"What are you doing?" Disgust races through me.

He doesn't answer me and starts to wipe my face. I push his hand away, and pain ignites in my side. The cloth touches my face again, and I don't have the power to stop him as he cleans me. I keep my eyes closed as his gentle strokes find their way deep inside me, stirring something that craves more. Kindness isn't something I've ever had around me.

I want him to stop. His gentle strokes are doing more damage than Oleg's violent ones. He stops like he read my mind. I still don't look as he lifts me and carries me to a radiator. I open my eyes in confusion as he lowers me to the carpeted ground. The click of the handcuff has me trying to pull away from the radiator. The Collector doesn't meet my eye. With stiff shoulders and controlled steps, he leaves the sitting room. The door closes and my body grows tired from holding in the pain and anger.

Oleg always liked them young. Liddi was sixteen going on sixty. At the mill, we shared a room. She was proud of what she was. She enjoyed sharing herself with men. I think it was the attention that she craved, the want to belong. Through the cracks, I could always see her damage.

I can picture her smiling at me as she lay on her bed, chewing gum. I kept getting requested. She was so proud, and my stomach rolled in disgust. Disgust that I knew was visible on my face.

"God, how did I end up sharing a room with someone like you?" She rolled onto her back, lifting her long tanned legs into the air. She had painted her nails a vibrant red. I turned away and continued to pick the wallpaper off the wall. I had the wall nearly bare; once I cleared it, I was going to paint. I smiled at the concrete slab.

"You are so weird. Why were you even sent here?" She said the same thing every few days.

It had been weeks, or had it been months since I was sent to the mill? I swallowed the bile. I had fought, but they'd dragged me here. From the first night, I had waited to be drugged or raped, but nothing happened. Killing myself was unsuccessful each time. I just never cut deep enough.

They placed Liddi in there with me, and she hated me so much. A year of sharing a cell with someone and never leaving, it did funny things to someone's mind. I wasn't given to anyone. I knew I should have been grateful for that small mercy. But sometimes listening to them cry out in fear or pain or even pleasure was worse than the act being done to me. I had to listen, and I couldn't change the outcome for any of these women.

Oleg visited Liddi often, and he was cruel and vicious with how he handled her. Her bruises coated most of her body, but she wore them like a badge of honor. Like it was something to be proud of.

I swallow the saliva that pools in my mouth and tug my arm again. The chains rattle against the radiator, and I want to scream again.

Oleg had stood over her, and she had said no, that she was tired. But you don't say no to a man like Oleg.

His slaps were delivered with his full force. I had never experienced the impact until now. My jaw still burns; my stomach throbs. I blink angry tears.

Liddi was stronger than most. Each slap he delivered, she took, and in retaliation, she laughed at him. I left the comfort of my bed and started to bang on the door for help, but no one came. I kept my back to them and felt along the wall until I reached the corner. It was there I hunkered down and covered my ears. I had listened to screams of pain before, just never that close, but my body responded like it always had, knowing I couldn't do anything, as if it were happening on the other side of the door.

Her laughter turned to screams, pleading with me to help her. I had been frozen to the spot, fear choking me. Then a scream pulled from deep inside me, and I screamed with her. I screamed long after Liddi stopped.

I tuck my face into the sleeve of my top and wipe some of the tears away. I lie there and hate where my mind keeps drifting to. Her screams haunt me.

I wake with a jolt. I know it's the middle of the night. A large hand covers my mouth. My gaze zooms in on The Collector. He uncuffs me, and he's so careful, making sure it doesn't rattle. His eyes meet mine again, and my stomach churns. His arms wrap around me, and he lifts me from the floor. I don't speak as he carries me from the sitting room and into the kitchen. Soft music plays as he carefully places me on the chair.

I'm aware of everywhere his hands touch and I hate that. I don't want to be aware of him. He leaves and I watch him make a sandwich. My stomach rumbles on cue as he places it in front of me. He hasn't spoken, but his eyes are roaring at me. They roam across my face, taking in each mark Oleg placed on my flesh. His eyes trail across my top, and I don't want to see what lies under it. He pushes the sandwich closer to me, and I pick it up and start to eat. Once I have half of the sandwich gone, I slow down.

"Thank you."

"How do you know Oleg?" His question has the bread turning heavy in the pit of my stomach.

"I don't." I close my eyes as I finish the other half of the sandwich.

"You're lying." The Collector lets out a heavy breath.

"Why are you feeding me?" I drop the sandwich onto the plate. His kindness is crueler than Oleg's.

"If you don't want to eat, then don't." He tries to sound like he doesn't care but fails.

I shift on the chair, and my side throbs. I grit my teeth until the pain passes. The Collector gets up and towers over me.

"Let me take a look."

"No." I hold my head high. He couldn't really help me.

"Mila." His warning has all my defenses dropping. It's the first time he's used my name. The understanding is visible in his eyes. He knows what he's doing. It's like naming a pet. Once you do, you get attached. Maybe that isn't a bad thing.

I let my hands hang at my side, and he steps in closer. His unique scent circles around me, and I reach out to steady myself.

"Ublyudok." He hisses the insult in Russian, and I agree with him. Oleg is a bastard. He touches my side and I inhale, sucking my flesh away from his fingers.

"I won't hurt you."

My gaze flickers to his. It's there on the tip of my tongue—*no, but you will let others hurt me.* I'm not his responsibility, and he owes me nothing, so my anger toward him is silly. I turn my head away as he continues to prod at my abdomen. It hurts, but nothing feels overly tender.

He seems satisfied and steps away. The loss of his warmth is immediate.

"Why does Victor want you?" The Collector asks the question like he doesn't really want the answer.

I close my eyes. Him knowing that won't do any good. Oleg's warning to keep what happened at the mill to myself still burns my flesh.

I shake my head. "I don't know." My lip trembles.

Time moves and when I look at The Collector, he nods. "Come on."

I leave the kitchen, and already, panic starts to grow about going back to the sitting room, back to my thoughts, which are like jagged glass.

When The Collector climbs the stairs, I'm climbing them right behind him. Anything to distract me and keep my thoughts at bay.

He takes me into the room with the four-poster bed. But he doesn't stop at the bed like I expect. I'm waiting for him to tell me to lie down so he can cuff me again, and it would be an improvement from the hard floor downstairs; he enters the bathroom and turns on the water. The blinds are up and the moon is high in the sky.

"Take a shower. I'll get you fresh clothes."

My gaze snaps to him. I want to thank him, but he leaves me. I enter the bathroom and start to strip off my clothes. Each movement is painful. My body aches and I refuse to look at myself in the mirror.

Movement behind me has me looking up. I meet a set of dark eyes in the mirror—eyes that burn with rage. Fear cuts off the air to my lungs. His gaze roams down the length of my body, and I follow in the mirror where his eyes trail along my flesh.

My heart pounds as I take in the damage Oleg did. My torso is painted in blacks and purples. My face is swollen on the left, yellow and red blossoms close to my hairline. There are dark circles under my eyes; I'm not sure if they're from Oleg or tiredness.

My hand curls around the counter as my heart threatens to leave my chest. Anger laces with shivers, and I close my eyes, cutting off the image of the battered girl. She looks just like someone I used to know. She reminds me of Liddi.

I keep my eyes on the ground as I step into the shower. I can't look at The Collector again. The spray of the water on my body has me tensing, and my tears mingle with the water as I gently wash my battered body.

CHAPTER ELEVEN

NICHOLAI

I CAN'T MOVE AS she steps away from the mirror and into the shower. Her body is black and blue. I release the T-shirt in my hand onto the bed. I want to go in there and look closer at her body; I want to let each mark sink in fully. I allowed that to happen.

I had no choice. I didn't know he was hurting her.

What else was Oleg or Victor going to do to her?

I walk over and close the blinds, trying not to pull them off the wall. Oleg bugged the room. The room Oleg had demanded I keep Mila locked in. They were listening for something. She was placed with me for a reason. She knows something. Are they waiting for her to reveal it to me? I run my hand down my face. Why would she reveal something to me? It makes no sense. The water stops running, and I hold firm and don't allow myself to enter the bathroom to tell her I'm sorry.

I glance at the watch on my wrist. It's three in the morning. She has a few more hours before I need to put her back in that room. Right now, they'll think she's asleep.

My gaze touches her as she steps into the bedroom wrapped in a single beige towel. Her blonde hair falls across her left shoulder. She looks so broken. I asked her how she knows Oleg, and she lied to me. I have to make her trust me. I have to find out why she was placed in my home, which is now bugged. Why did she deny knowing Oleg? What do they think they'll hear between us?

I speak up. "My mother used to always say, 'Don't blame a mirror for your ugly face.'"

Mila stares at me, and her cheeks redden under the bruises.

I take a step toward her, holding up a hand. "I'm not saying you're ugly. In fact, you're beautiful."

She inhales a large gulp of air, making her chest rise. A ghost of a smile plays on her lips. "What does it mean then?" she asks.

It's a question. One question leads to two, and then I won't be able to stop it. I could let her get dressed and return her to the sitting room and let her wait for Oleg to come back and collect her. That's the end result. There's no point in entertaining this. She will be collected. Everyone is.

Her blue eyes swim with what looks like hope, and she tightens her small fists around the towel before taking a step toward me.

"She was telling me not to blame others for my own mistakes. I got into this line of work because of my father and uncle. Being the only son and nephew, it was a path I was determined to follow. Even against my mother's wishes."

Mila's eyes are wide, like she can't believe I'm sharing, and that makes me smile. For now, I'll allow this.

"But when I told her that, she replied with 'Don't blame a mirror for your ugly face.' It's stuck with me." I can't stop the smile. I loved my mother, but she had a wicked tongue. Even as she aged and I grew taller, overshadowing her, she was still formidable. She still dictated from the end of the table, always trying to guide me in the right direction.

"You're a good boy, Nicholai. Be a good boy."

"She sounds wise." Mila's voice is small and soft.

"Yeah, she was. I should have listened to her." Regret at taking this job surprises not just me but Mila too.

Her eyes widen again. Goose bumps rise along her arms, and I drop the jogging pants on the bed beside the T-shirt. Her eyes jump to the clothes on the bed.

"I thought you might need something clean."

She tightens her hold on the towel again. "Thank you."

Her words are soft, and I don't want to hear them. I know if I hadn't collected her, some other collector would have. Whatever she did had caused this all to spin into motion.

"When you're dressed, come downstairs to the kitchen. Try to be quiet. I think they're listening to us."

Her color fades, and she nods like she expected something like this to happen. Her gaze moves to the floor. I wonder... now that I have shared with her, will she share with me?

I'm quiet downstairs, and just to be careful, I turn up the music. I take out my phone and check the tracker. She's coming down the hall, but she's paused. No good can come from this. I try to talk myself off a ledge as I stare at the red dot. I wait and count to ten before she starts to move, and I close the phone as she comes down the stairs.

She looks unsure as she enters the kitchen.

I need to make her comfortable. The need in me to understand this has me pointing at the chair. "Sit down. I'll get you a drink."

My T-shirt and jogging pants look good on her. I pour both of us a shot of vodka. She takes it and swigs it down quickly before she starts to cough. I wait until she stops and drink my own.

"They placed bugs in the sitting room and demanded that you be kept locked up in there at all times."

Her nostrils flare, and her long fingers tighten on the glass.

"Why would they do that?" I ask.

I don't stare at her but get up and take the bottle of vodka off the counter and bring it back to the table. I fill hers and then mine. She drinks hers and coughs again, but it's more controlled.

"First time drinking," she says when she stops coughing. She rubs her mouth with the back of her hand.

"Why's that?"

She looks away from me. "Strict parents."

"My father gave me my first drink when I was eight." I share again, hoping to open her up. I was pissed out of my mind that night. All I remember is my father's and uncle's faces meshing together before I passed out. I woke to my mother flinging a bucket of water over me. She was mad. Mad enough to fire the bucket at me once I was awake.

She doesn't speak, staring into her empty glass. She's hiding something. There's no doubt about it.

I refill her glass and knock mine back before refilling my own. "Why don't we play a game?"

Her head shoots up to me.

She looks like I'm going to eat her. "I ask a question and then you ask a question. Whoever doesn't answer has to take a shot."

"Isn't that what we're doing?" She's weary.

"Yeah, I suppose it is," I answer.

"How long have you been The Collector?" Her question makes me smile. We're getting somewhere. She's interested and that will keep her here.

"I was twenty-four when I got the job. So eight years."

Her gaze skims across my face and down to my neck. "How long were you in prison?"

I smile. "It's my turn," I remind her, and she tucks her chin into her chest. I decide to start with something easy. "How long did you work at the café?"

Her shoulders relax. "Six years. I was so lucky when I met Elena and she offered me the job."

Her gaze takes on a far off look. I wonder if she's thinking of the old life she had to leave behind. Dimitri's daughter comes to mind, and I drink down the shot.

"I didn't ask you anything yet." Her smile is refreshing.

I refill my glass. "Yeah, go ahead."

"What was the first collection like?"

I thought she would go back to the question about prison. That seemed easier than this one.

"The hardest." I twirl the glass in my hand. I could drink and not answer. That's the game, but within the game, we're playing a game.

"I threw up," I admit.

Her lip tugs down slightly. "Why?" she whispers, and that's a second question.

"That's two questions," I remind her, and she sits back.

"Before the café, where did you work?"

Her jaw tightens and she glances at the glass.

Don't pick it up.

I'm hoping she trusts me enough to share something real about herself.

CHAPTER TWELVE

MILA

I WANT TO GET to know him, but I'm not sure if the price tag is too high. It isn't a hard question; it's more about where it could lead. But no matter the question, each of them carries their own weight.

"I didn't work," I answer.

His clenched jaw doesn't go unnoticed.

"What happens when you collect someone?" I ask and he sits back. I'm not being fair. He's giving me more than he's receiving, but I'm trying to give him everything he needs.

"I drop them at the can. It's a small building. I leave them there, and then that's it."

I'm sitting forward. "What do you mean, that's it?"

He pauses and I curse myself. It's two questions.

"That's it. Someone else picks them up."

"Like a delivery service?" I ask before I drink to try to quench my anger, but it's fuel to the fire.

"How do you know Oleg?"

I pick up my empty glass and twirl it in my hand. "I don't want to go back into the room." I look up at The Collector.

He glances at his watch. "We don't have much more time."

My heart bounces around in my chest as The Collector fills my glass. "I was in the mill," I say, and the vodka overflows from the glass and across my hand.

His reaction has shame burning my face.

"Sorry." He gets up and grabs a towel.

I can't decipher what's going through his mind as he starts to dab away at my hand.

When he sits down, he knocks back his vodka before his dark eyes flicker to my face.

"I've heard of the mill."

I snort a laugh, but it holds no humor. "Who hasn't?" I even knew of it before Victor put me in it—a lesson he wanted to teach me.

"Is that how you know Oleg?" His question has me shaking my head.

"What does it matter? How do you know they didn't bug your kitchen?" I could tell him how I know Oleg, but that knowledge might bring a mess down on him, and I don't want that.

"I've checked the kitchen and it isn't bugged. How you know Oleg does matter. I'm trying to understand all this." He speaks through gritted teeth.

"Yes, I knew him from the mill." My voice is low, and saying it out loud has my throat and eyes burning. I can't look at The Collector. His lips are starting to curl up, no doubt in disgust but for all the wrong reasons.

I glance at him, and the level of anger in his eyes undoes me.

"I wasn't with him." My chest heats.

He doesn't speak.

"He used to visit my roommate. Liddi." I bite my lip to keep the emotions in. I didn't think it would be this hard. I smile and my vision blurs. "I don't want to talk anymore."

I drop my gaze and wipe a lone tear that runs down my cheek. The Collector doesn't move and I look up at him.

"I'm ready to go back to the sitting room." My lips tug down, and he fills up my glass, but I shake my head. I don't want to play anymore. He has no idea.

"Do you believe a cat has nine lives?" The Collector asks the question like it's relevant.

"I don't know. Do you?"

"No," he answers before drinking down another vodka.

I drink my own. "Now you have to explain why you asked that."

"Three for playing, three for straying, and three for staying. That's what their nine lives added up to, or so their story went. I often wondered if I got nine lives, how I would live each." He pours out another shot, and I wonder if he is getting drunk.

That thought is sobering. Never mind nine more lives—just one more. A do-over. What would I do differently?

"If I could do it again," I start, and blink at the table, "I would have been stronger." No matter how many times I'm reborn, I will be reborn into the same family, but if I was stronger, that is what could make the difference. My gaze flickers up to The Collector.

"I think you are so much stronger than you think." His smile is soft, and my heart pounds at the kindness in his eyes. His gaze flickers to the shot of vodka before he refocuses on me. "You survived the mill."

I hear the unspoken question. *How?* The opinion of the girls in the mill is the same across the board. He, no doubt, thinks I'm a whore.

After giving him a blowjob, I don't blame him. I drop his gaze and down the shot of vodka.

"I didn't survive the mill." I tap the glass on the table as the vodka burns my throat.

Silence drowns us in the kitchen.

"I better get you back." He sounds unsure, and this time he doesn't meet my eye. I'm grateful for the vodka; it's numbed some of the pain.

I don't look at The Collector as he cuffs me to the radiator. I don't make a sound and neither does he, but when the cuffs are back on my wrist, he still doesn't move. I dare take a peek at him. Dark eyes send my stomach fluttering. He reaches out and gently touches my bruised face. His jaw tightens and he stands, leaving me alone again with my thoughts.

I expect my mind to go to the mill—it's what's haunted me for the last six years. Instead, my mind goes further back.

Strobe lights from the club bounce off Eric as he dances. He sticks his tongue out at me, and I'm running through the crowd. He follows me as I knew he would. We break through and end up outside. Rain pelts down, but we don't care.

There are no boundaries when I'm with Eric. I'm free to do what I want. He is the air my family refused to give me. His laughter is poured into the night sky before he looks around him. His blue eyes twinkle, and I know we're about to do something crazy. His large hand wraps around my small one, and we're running down the small street. Eric looks at me again, and his smile is infectious.

"What are we doing?" I ask through my smile. I don't care. I'd follow him off a cliff. He knows that. He stops at a Porsche and his elbow smashes into the glass. The alarm sounds and deep down I know

this isn't right. We could get into serious trouble. He pulls the door open and jumps in, but I'm staring at his blond head.

"Get in, Mila."

His voice is alarmed, and I can hear the sirens in the distance. I jump in and he gets the car started. The rush as we tear through the small streets has me screaming in joy. Eric blares the music, and both of us are lost in the thrill of the moment. Both of us are high on adrenaline.

"Oh fuck."

I glance out the back window to see four squad cars following us. I'm laughing. I'm dead if they catch us. My laughter has Eric laughing too, and we're moving faster. Everything is blurring around me, and I want to hang out the window and let the wind whip past me. I want to fly. I want to be free.

My heart roars as I wake up from the memory. The room is dark, and I'm searching the space for Eric's blue eyes. They were so alive, so vibrant. I squeeze my eyes and his face dissolves. Tears burn my throat, and I curl closer to the radiator. The vodka still burns through my veins and sends me into another sleep. One that's quiet this time.

CHAPTER THIRTEEN

NICHOLAI

I WAKE UP TO a noise in the house. I can't figure out exactly what it is, but I know it doesn't belong. I slept above the covers. Oleg's words of seeing us again kept me vigilant. I'm mentally checking myself. I have my gun strapped to my ankle. The throwing knives are on my wrists. I open the top drawer of my bedside table and remove another gun and click off the safety.

The house is dark, and I pause in the hall and take out my phone. Mila is still in the sitting room. Her dot is unmoving. That gives me some ease. I move to the edge of the wall and peek out across the stairs. The hall is silent. I close my eyes and listen again.

Someone is in the house. They're downstairs. The sound comes from the back of the house, and I move down the stairs soundlessly. I open the door, needing to confirm what my phone told me. Mila is still tied to the radiator. She's asleep. Her chest rises and falls. I pull the door closed and release a knife as a shadow skitters across the hall.

The scream is instant, and I withdraw my gun as I zigzag down the hall. I reach the man who's coated in black. He's trying to pull the knife from his shoulder. I cock the gun at his head and he freezes.

"Are you alone?" I'm looking all around me.

"Yes."

The lie has me moving quickly, as the attack comes from behind me. A second man, also dressed in black. I remove the second knife and swipe quickly. He freezes, but I felt the contact. He gargles as his hands reach for his open throat. It only takes three more seconds until he hits the ground.

"Are you alone?" I ask again.

"I am now." He's telling the truth.

"Who sent you?"

He's wearing a balaclava. I want to see the man's face who broke into my home and tried to kill me. He moves quicker than expected. The gun appears and I kick it out of his hand. It hits the floor with a thud but doesn't fire. I spin him, wrapping my arm around his neck. His fists swing back, but I tighten my hold. He keeps fighting, but it dwindles. I release him and his dead body hits the floor.

I move quickly back to the sitting room door and open it. Mila is still asleep. I didn't want the bugs to pick up on the noise. My first thought is that Oleg sent them. I'm not sure if it was to kill me or Mila, but either way, both men now lie dead in my hallway.

I search the remainder of the house. It's clear. The back door is open. It was a simple job. They picked the locks. I check the camera outside for the gates, which are still closed. They scaled the walls. I never had a security system installed. I never had to. No one was stupid enough to come to my home—that is, until now.

I check both bodies for IDs, but they aren't carrying anything. After that, I examine their bodies for markings. They both have tattoos, but none that are significant. Blood pools in the hall. I pull my knife from the shoulder of the man I strangled before getting plastic and wrapping both bodies. Once I have them tied, I drag them into the garage and heave both of them into the trunk of my car.

This time when I check on Mila, she's awake. The sun has started to rise, casting shadows on her face. I nod at her and she nods back. I hate closing the door, but I can't go near her until tonight. It takes a few attempts to get the blood off my floor, but I finally do.

I don't want to leave Mila, but I can't imagine whoever sent these men would send more so soon. Leaving now would be wiser than later.

I drive out as far as the can. It's barren out here. After placing both bodies on the ground, I douse them in petrol and drop a match. They go up in flames straight away. Would Oleg have sent them? I have no idea why he would want me dead. Killing off Mila might make sense since she knows something. She's hiding something. Tonight, I need her to trust me. I need to find out what secret this girl is carrying.

I return to the house and shower before eating. I replace the locks and go back upstairs to sleep the day away. I lie on the covers again. My guns are ready. Checking my phone before I fall asleep, I make sure Mila is where she should be. She is.

She eats all the spaghetti on her plate, and when she finally looks up at me, her cheeks grow red. "I'm hungry."

"You want more?" I ask.

She shakes her head. "I could use some of that vodka."

I don't want her to get drunk, but I can understand the appeal, especially if she never drank before. It numbed a lot of the pain this world threw at us. I get two shot glasses and fill both of them before I return to the table.

She reaches out and then knocks it back, and her face scrunches up as she swallows the liquid.

"I'll have another."

I hesitate but fill the glass.

"Two men broke into the house last night," I tell her and drink the shot. I'm watching her more carefully than I ever have.

"What? Did they steal anything?" She blinks several times.

"They came to kill me, or maybe you."

Her nostrils flare as she scrambles for air while shaking her head. "Me? But..." she stutters and looks away.

"I can't help you if I don't know what I'm up against."

Her gaze springs to me. "Help me?" She shakes her head again, but hope blossoms in her blue eyes. "I don't know anyone who would want me dead."

The lie has me refilling my glass. I'm getting nowhere with her. I'm staring at her, wondering when she will crack, but she stares right back.

"Let's go for a drive."

Her eyes widen and she stands up at the idea of getting out. I give her the shoes she arrived in and a pair of my socks. I hand her one of my jackets, which she drowns in, and we leave the house. I keep taking peeks at her as she watches the world move past. It's pitch black, but she's staring up at the sky. It's dotted with stars.

I drive into the city, and the light pours from windows and flashing neon signs. I drive past Gail's and keep moving through the city.

"Where are we going?" It's the first time she's asked the question.

"I want to show you something." I hope it will help her open up a bit more. I leave the city behind and keep driving as the landscape grows barren. When we pull up at the can, the ground is scorched from burning the bodies. It's a pile of ashes.

"Stay in the car," I tell her as I get out and take a shovel from the boot. I dig a large hole to the left of the scorched ground and scoop in all the ashes and remains of the bodies. Digging up the burnt soil, I turn it. When I feel satisfied, I return the shovel to the car before moving to the passenger door. Mila swallows when I open it.

"Come on, I want to show you something."

Her fingers tighten around the belt. "Are you going to kill me?"

"No. I want to show you where I drop people off." I reach in and relish the smell of her. It's my shower gel, but underneath it is something sweet, like vanilla. I unclip her belt, and I don't want to lean out. I inhale before I do.

She gets out hesitantly and follows me over to the can. I open the door and she doesn't step closer.

"Look in, Mila."

The pulse in her neck pounds, but she steps up to the door and peeks in before quickly moving back, like I might push her in.

"I drop the people off here. They wait until they are collected. It could be hours or even days. Can you imagine waiting in that small cell?"

"Why are you showing me this?" Her voice wavers.

"Because this is your fate."

She shakes her head like she might be able to change it.

"It doesn't have to be like this," I say. "Let me help you."

She laughs. "You want to help me?"

"Yes."

"Why?"

It's a good question. Why do I feel this need to save her? "If you want to end up in the can, then that's fine, Mila."

I'm ready to walk away, but she doesn't follow.

"Even if I told you, you can't protect me." She sounds so defeated, and I pause before turning back to her.

"Try me." I start to walk back to her, but I see in her eyes she's not ready to talk.

"Oleg..." She swallows and looks away. "Just take me back to the house."

Disappointment and frustration course through me, and I laugh at her.

"You were right," I say with a smirk.

"What?" She's shaking as she wraps her arms across her chest.

"I wish you were stronger too."

She is strong, but if I poke, she might crack. She doesn't, as she walks back to the car, keeping her secrets firmly against her chest.

CHAPTER FOURTEEN

MILA

I GLANCE AT THE freshly turned soil and wonder exactly what he's covering up. There's a smell in the air that makes my stomach turn. I've smelled it before. Burnt flesh.

I get into the car, and The Collector gets in and starts the engine. Telling him about Oleg won't do me any good. The more The Collector knows, the further he will run from me.

I could lie, tell him I was a mill girl who escaped, but he could see through my lies. I thought of telling him about what I saw Oleg do, but that wouldn't solve this problem. He can't stop this. No one can.

I try to take in the city as we move past it. There's something beautiful about the nighttime. It always makes me believe that anything is possible. Eric made me feel that way. Like we could jump from a cliff and land on our feet.

I glance at The Collector. His hands are tight around the steering wheel. I have no idea if he's really trying to help me, or if maybe Oleg is testing me to see if I will tell The Collector. They could be working together. That seems far more likely than the fantasy of him trying to save me from the bad man.

"Can we walk around the city?" I ask, not expecting it to happen. The car slows down under us, and The Collector pulls up along some run-down buildings. His Audi looks out of place here, but he doesn't seem to notice.

We get out and walk toward the more lit-up part of the city.

"Do you have siblings?" I ask him.

He stuffs his hands into his trouser pockets. "Why do you always wear a suit?" I fire. He looks handsome, but I've only ever once seen him in formal clothes.

"I'm always on the clock so I'm ready for work, and no, I don't have any siblings." He doesn't look at me as he speaks.

Always on the clock. Has he no personal life? The Collector is a mystery to most people. I've always seen him as someone ruthless and uncaring. But that's not the man walking beside me.

"Don't you ever get lonely?" I ask.

His smirk has my face growing warm. "No." He's looking at me from the corner of his eye, and heat races down my chest.

I don't like the idea of any other woman touching him, and the jealousy that courses through me makes me stumble.

He pauses. "Are you okay?"

He seems so sincere. What if he really wants to help me? I haven't felt this way about anyone in a long time. A part of me is saying I should take a leap of faith. I might land on my feet.

Or you could land on your ass, Mila.

"Mila," he says, and it brings me back to him.

"I don't even know your name."

"Nicholai," he offers up.

My stomach squirms. "Nicholai," I repeat, and he smiles, but I don't. I'm going to say something I can't take back. "I witnessed something." His smile vanishes, and his body grows tense.

"I saw Oleg kill someone." I'm leaning in while whispering. Fear has my heart pounding. I hope I haven't made a mistake in sharing this with him.

He frowns. "Who?"

"Liddi." Her name is painful to say. "She was a kid." I look away from Nicholai. "I was there."

Nicholai touches my arm. "Was she someone important?"

She was to someone, I suppose. But I know what he's asking me. I shake my head. "No."

Nicholai nods and we continue to walk again. I don't know if he can see it in my eyes—I'm not giving up anymore. Even telling him that is dangerous. It isn't because Liddi was important; it's because I am.

I glance at Nicholai.

"Nicholai." I try out his name again, and he gives me a sidelong glance.

"It suits you," I finish.

His lip tugs up, and my heart races a little faster. I reach for his arm and link mine with his. He doesn't stop me, but I'm a little unsteady right now.

"Don't say anything."

I look up at Nicholai, but he's staring at a woman who approaches us. Her brown eyes flicker to me, and I want to disappear.

"Nicholai, how are you?" She squeezes his arm with a hand clad in red leather. I release Nicholai, and I want to step away.

"Who is this?" she's asking while looking at me. I know how I must appear in Nicholai's too large jacket, my face bruised and swollen. "You poor child! What happened to you?"

"What can I do for you?"

Nicholai's voice has the woman's spine straightening and her smile slips. Perfectly arched eyebrows rise high into the air as she stares at him with a hate I'm accustomed to seeing.

"Can't an old friend greet another?"

I tighten my fists, which are hidden under the sleeves of Nicholai's jacket.

"I'm busy, Gail." He turns to me and I follow him, but not before I meet Gail's assessing eyes. She's curious. I shiver as I pass her and follow Nicholai.

"Who was she?" I ask, glancing over my shoulder at her as she continues her walk down the street. Her red heels click along the sidewalk. She's a very well put together woman.

"No one."

Now he has my attention. "She said she was a friend." I don't know why I'm getting jealous.

"She lied." He glances at me now, and I don't like how he's lying to me.

"I don't care if she's your girlfriend," I say offhandedly.

Nicholai stops walking and he's in front of me. He's angry and I have no idea why. He looks like he has hundreds of words strung together before he dismantles them.

"We better get back." He jogs across the road, and I have a fleeting thought of running when I look down the street. If I ran, how far would I get?

Not far, my brain tells me as I follow him to the car.

When we arrive back at the house, Nicholai tells me to wait in the car until he checks the house. He takes the keys out of the ignition, but I feel itchy sitting in a car alone. All I want to do is drive away.

His garage is in perfect order. A shelf to the left holds three tins of paint, all front facing. Below them is a roll of plastic and to the left, a red tool box. Below it are boxes that are sealed up. That's it—the space is clear of everything else. Even his car is spotless. I glance at the door before I pop the glove compartment. I have no idea what I'm looking for.

A scream falls from my lips. Nicholai taps on the window; he's staring straight at me. I close the glove compartment and climb out of the car. When I meet his eye, I'm tempted to apologize but I don't. We enter the kitchen and music plays. I want to know how much time I have before I have to go back to the room.

I want more vodka. I want to slip into that numb state where I dream but it doesn't tear at me. I'm about to ask when Nicholai pours out two shots. I can't stop the smile as I shrug out of his jacket. He watches me walk across the space and pick up the shot. I'm ready to knock it back, but something in his eyes stops me.

"What?" I ask. Is it poisoned?

He takes the shot out of my hand and reaches around me, placing it on the table. He's so close, and my body responds to his closeness. His large hand grips the back of my neck, and I can't breathe as he presses his lips to mine. His lips are warm, and I open my mouth, allowing his tongue access. His hand tightens on my neck, pulling me closer. My breasts smash against his hard chest, and for the first time, I want to see every inch of this man. His jacket hits the floor, and I easily push off his waistcoat too. He breaks the kiss, and I think he's going to stop this.

"Come on," he says.

I follow him upstairs and excitement bubbles through my veins. I inhale deeply as we enter the room with the four-poster bed. I step up to it, and wetness pools between my legs at the thought of having him on top of me, in me.

His cock was huge in my mouth. What would it feel like inside me? I close my eyes when his hands touch the bottom of my top. I raise my hands in the air as he pulls it off. His breath fans out along my neck, and my nipples grow hard immediately. I groan when his long fingers roll the nipples, sending waves of pleasure throughout my system. His large cock pushes against my ass, and I bite my lip. Having my back to him makes me braver, and I move my ass against his cock.

His groan has me grinning and he spins me. He's removed his shirt, and his body is all artwork. My heart beats wildly, and fear starts to crawl along my skin. Sleeping with The Collector would be one of the dumbest ideas I've ever had. His lips slam down on mine, erasing any doubts I'm having.

We move back onto the bed, and I open my eyes, staring up at the mirror above us. His back is covered in tattoos. A black cross runs down the full length of his spine. His back shifts and moves, making the images look alive. My core throbs, and I look away from the image and into dark eyes that threaten to consume me.

CHAPTER FIFTEEN

NICHOLAI

IT'S HARD NOT TAKING her quickly. Even with bruises on her face and body, she's still gorgeous. There's an air about her, something I can't put my finger on, but I want to know more about her. She's intriguing me. I move us up the bed until her head rests on the pillows. Her small breasts are free, and they are perfect.

She's glancing up at the mirror again, and I grin as I slip out of my trousers and boxers. Her gaze flickers to me, and her chest rises and falls fast as I remove everything. Her expression has me crawling back to her. Her blue eyes search mine, and the lust that swims in them has my cock growing harder. Her jogging pants slip off easily, and she's not wearing any underwear. Her legs separate under my hands, and her head falls back onto the pillow as I place a kiss on the inside of her thigh.

My cock wants to fuck her hard, but I take my time. Her pussy is wet; the liquid shines on the inside of her thighs. I stretch her legs further and glance up at her before I press my mouth to her pussy.

She arches while groaning, her hands automatically going to my hair. I sink my tongue in as far as it can go and swirl it inside her sweet pussy. Gripping her thighs, I push her legs back as far as possible. She tastes so sweet. I remove my mouth and dip a finger inside her. Her hands leave my hair, and I look up at her. Her eyes swirl with lust. I insert a second and third finger, stretching her for my cock.

"I want to see you," I say, as I push all three fingers inside her. She arches again, and I slowly pull my fingers out.

"I want to see you in the mirror," I say, lying down.

She's up on her knees, and I grab all that blonde hair so I can see her as she takes my cock into her mouth. Her warm mouth moves down it and slides back up. Her mouth feels better than the first time.

I tighten my hold on her hair and push her head down again. She takes more of my cock into her sweet mouth. Her mouth is warm and small, but she moves down as far as she can go. I want more of her. Pulling her head up, she wipes her mouth with the back of her hand. I want to fuck her from behind. I want to hold her hair as I pound my cock into her.

She's breathing heavily, waiting for what I want to do next.

"Get on all fours."

She bites her lip at my command, and I grip her hips, pulling her back toward my throbbing cock. Her pussy is soaking, and I dip the head of my cock inside her. She throws her head back, her hair flicking out across her back. I gather it up and grip it as I ease further into her. She cries out as her tight pussy clenches around my cock. I push further in, and it feels so fucking good. Running my thumb along her ass, which is wet as well, I'm tempted to pull my cock from her pussy and fuck that tight ass.

I push fully into her pussy and dip my thumb inside her ass. She cries out, and I slowly pull out of both holes before moving back in. My cock stretches her further, and she feels perfect around me. I dip more of my thumb into her ass, and her groans encourage me to go faster and deeper. The walls of her pussy swell around me, and I move my cock faster, pushing my thumb fully into her ass. I move it around as I fuck her pussy hard. Her groans and cries have my release rising quickly. I pound faster, loving the sound of our flesh slapping against each other. I push my thumb deeper inside her ass and she cries out.

"Nicholai."

My name falling from her lips in pleasure has me moving faster. My cock throbs. Her ass is soaking and clenches around my finger. I sense her pussy clenching as I drive my cock as fast and hard as I can into her. She screams her release, and I pour my seed inside her. I keep pounding until I'm completely emptied. She's gasping for air when I remove my finger from her ass and cock from her pussy. She rolls over onto her back. Her face is flushed and she looks perfect.

I roll onto my own back and meet her eyes in the overhead mirror. Her smile has me smiling. Her body fits perfectly against mine. Her pussy fits perfectly around my cock. She doesn't seem like a girl who just came from the mill. She was tight; she was fresh. She wasn't a virgin, but I don't think she was that far off it.

"What's wrong?" she asks, still breathless.

I shake my head. "Nothing is wrong. Nothing at all. You were very loud."

Her cheeks heat up, but she smiles.

"I hope no one heard you"—I smile—"screaming my name."

"I wasn't exactly screaming it."

I raise a brow and look away from the mirror so I can look at her beside me. "You were screaming my name and I liked it."

I kiss her before getting up. I hate doing this, but she needs to go back to her room. Meeting Gail was also another complication I'm not happy with. The way she looked at Mila... I need to be more careful where I take her. Taking her out like that was stupid of me.

After I wash myself down, I return to the room. Mila is still sprawled out on the bed. She isn't asleep. She's staring at herself in the mirror. Her eyes skim across each bruise.

"You are beautiful," I tell her.

Her gaze bounces to me. She snorts. "I'm a mess."

I take a step toward her and see that flicker of fear in her eyes. "Bruises will fade. Your beauty won't."

She looks away from me, her brow furrowed. I need to get her back to her room. I pull on my boxers and trousers.

"It's getting close to morning," I say.

Mila sits up on the bed, and I pass her my T-shirt and jogging pants. She pulls them on.

"Do you know when they will come for me?"

"No." I can't look at her. I pull on my shirt. I have no idea what I'm going to do. I will cross that bridge when I come to it, I suppose.

She gets dressed and I walk her downstairs. This is the worst I've felt. She pauses at the door. I have no idea what to say to her. She doesn't linger but walks into the room. She sits on the floor, and I cuff her again. I pause and touch her face. She leans her cheek into my touch, and I get up and leave her alone again.

CHAPTER SIXTEEN

MILA

I can't sleep and I have no vodka in my system to knock me out. I start to sing. I'm tone deaf, but I'm thinking whoever is listening in will want to tune it out. I sing every song I can think of. I miss most of the words but make up my own. The song is ridiculous, but I start to enjoy myself, knowing I'm pissing someone off.

It's not close to the kick I used to feel with Eric. When we were together, we were nothing but trouble. I was always on a high with him. We normally did something inappropriate, but in my world of rules and men, letting loose wasn't acceptable, especially not for a girl. Eric could do what he wanted, and he did, but when they discovered I was with him breaking all the rules, they locked me up in the mill to teach me a lesson.

My fist tightens into a ball. At first, I really believed Eric would come rescue me. But he never did.

I wake to an empty room. I'm not sure what time it is, but it's still dark. I feel like it's always dark when I sleep and when I wake. I can't seem to separate the day from night. Too much joy bounces around inside me when the door opens, but it melts away as a man dressed in black steps into the room. I push myself deeper into the radiator. My chains rattle and he raises a black-gloved finger to his mouth, telling me to be silent. I'm ready to scream for Nicholai when he moves closer to me, but fear closes my throat.

I can't see his face as he kneels down and touches the handcuffs. A second figure moves into the room, and this one has everything in me growing still.

Nicholai moves up behind the man soundlessly, and his arm tightens around his neck. A small noise leaves the man's lips, but it's cut off as Nicholai tightens his hold. The man starts to claw and move slightly forward. Nicholai is going to kill him if he doesn't let him go. My heart races and I'm moving again. Nicholai's eyes clash with mine, and I hope mine are screaming my thoughts. I know not to speak, but he's killing him.

"Let him go," I mouth as my throat grows dry.

The man continues to swing at Nicholai, who moves him further away from me. I'm shaking my head as the man fights for his last breath and loses. His body grows limp in Nicholai's arms, and he drags him out of the room. The door closes, and I'm left wondering if that even just happened. If I just watched the light leave the man's eyes.

My heart won't stop jumping at every little sound. I'm waiting for someone to storm the room but no one does. What's going on? Is there more than one person? Is Nicholai okay? I tug at my handcuffs while holding the chain to try to keep the noise level down. After a moment, I abandon the notion to stay quiet and rattle the chains. Using both feet, I push against the radiator and try to break the chain—to no avail.

"Nicholai!" I scream. I'm ready to scream again when he enters the room, his gun out. He's looking at everything but me.

When his gaze meets mine, I shake my head to say no one is here. He puts away the gun, and his brow furrows as he unlocks my aching wrists.

Once we leave the sitting room, he steers me into the kitchen and slams the door before turning up the music to a ridiculous level.

"Don't ever use my name again." He's so close to me. The anger that laces through his words startles me, and I take a step back.

"I thought..." I don't finish my sentence.

"You know Oleg is listening. What will he think when you're screaming my name?"

I can't breathe with him this close. I take another step back. "I don't know. That I was hungry or something."

"Then you shout for 'The Collector.' Otherwise, it sounds personal." His voice lowers and his eyes soften, but I still feel the sting of him reprimanding me.

"I'll remember that in the future," I say and look away from him.

Everything in me freezes. I don't know how I hadn't seen the two bodies before, lying close to the back door. A sheet of plastic under them is stopping the blood that oozes from one man onto the tiled floor. I can't look away as the walls seem to close in around me.

"Are they dead?" I ask Nicholai, but I don't take my eyes off the men. The blood oozes and pools, sending shivers racing across my skin. He strangled one man and didn't pause in taking his life. Liddi's screams begging me to help her haunt me now as I watch the blood expand.

"She screamed so loudly," I say as my throat burns. I cover my mouth with my hand to try to keep in the words that want to pour. "She begged me to help her." My breaths grow ragged as I stare at the bodies. "She begged me." I blink and the room spins at the confession. "I covered my ears to stop her screams." Shame burns deep inside me, and I finally look at Nicholai, who watches me.

"My screams covered hers." Salty liquid enters my mouth, and I lick my tearstained lips.

Nicholai walks over to me and grips my arms in his large hands—hands that just took a life. I shrug him off.

"I did nothing for her," I admit and wipe my face.

"I can't help you right now, Mila. I need you to be strong." He nods and grips my arms again. "Can you be strong for me?" His brows rise as he waits for my answer. He's asking me not to fall apart right now.

I nod. "Yes."

He releases me and returns to the bodies on the ground. Kneeling down, he starts to search through their pockets, but he comes up with nothing. I take a step closer. Nicholai pulls off the balaclava, and the man's face is younger than I expected.

My stomach twists. His bloodshot eyes are open, staring up at the ceiling, bulging. Nicholai moves his head from left to right and pauses. I step closer. A small tattoo of an octopus behind his ear looks funny. Nicholai curses in Russian again. He searches the other body, but he has no tattoos or markings.

"Does his tattoo have a meaning?" I ask.

Nicholai stays hunkered and runs his hands across his face before his dark eyes bore into me. "Yes."

My stomach twists. It must have to do with Oleg. He wants me dead. He wants his secret buried with me too.

"It's personal," Nicholai says, and something that feels like relief swims through me.

He pulls the plastic over the first body, and the man's face disappears. I stay where I am as Nicholai lifts the body out of the kitchen and into the garage.

I'm staring at the second body, which still oozes blood. I'm too close. My stomach lifts and I quickly walk away. Opening cupboards, I find the bottle of vodka and drink straight from it. The path it burns down my throat settles me a bit.

The rustling of plastic has me glancing over at Nicholai as he wraps the second body and takes it from the kitchen. It's like no one was even here. I take another long swallow of the vodka before reluctantly putting the cap back on.

When Nicholai returns to the kitchen, his gaze lands on me. His tight jaw and stiff shoulders have me putting the bottle down.

"Come on." He doesn't wait for me to respond but leaves through the garage door. I make a last-minute decision and bring the bottle of vodka with me.

We drive through the city again, and my brain keeps looping to the fact there are two dead bodies in the trunk of the car. I peek at Nicholai several times. He works a muscle in his jaw. I don't ask why someone would want him dead. It sounds like a stupid question.

"Does this happen often?" I ask.

Nicholai's eyes bounce from the bottle of vodka tucked between my legs to my eyes.

"No." His answer is abrupt.

I can't focus as he runs his thumb across his lips in thought. Right now, I know I shouldn't be thinking about how gorgeous he is. Right now, I should be far more concerned about the bodies in the car. I unscrew the lid and take another drink of vodka. I'm waiting for Nicholai to say something about me drinking, but he doesn't.

We drive out as far as the can, and now I think of the turned-over soil from before. Nicholai gets out and I wonder how many bodies are buried here. I know if he hadn't killed the men, they would have killed him, maybe even me. But it still doesn't stop the uneasy feeling spreading through my veins.

I drink again as he drags the bodies in front of the headlights of the car. I'm ready to throw up when he douses them in petrol. Did they have families? Children? A wife waiting at home for them to return?

He drops the match and Nicholai's face is cast in light and shadows. His gaze meets mine in the car, and I don't know if it's just me, but I see it. I've witnessed a murder. I've watched him burn the bodies, and no doubt they will be buried here just like the others. The reminder of the smell of burnt flesh from earlier has me drinking again.

Nicholai walks to the passenger side and opens the door. He leans in, and my heart leaps into my throat. His fingers brush mine as he removes the bottle of vodka from my hands and takes a large drink before handing it back. I press my lips to it and drink down more.

We both share the bottle as we watch the bodies burn. We drink in silence, each of us lost in our own thoughts.

CHAPTER SEVENTEEN

NICHOLAI

Mila just witnessed me killing and burning two men; therefore, I can't leave her in the house on her own. No doubt Gail would send more men. Gail must have been pretty pissed over Dimitri to send men to kill me. I hadn't thought her so foolish.

The sun is starting to rise, and I need to get Mila back. She's tipsy, and maybe that isn't a bad thing. Her wild eyes bounce around the space, and I have no idea what's going through her mind, but I have no doubt she's terrified right now.

She's smiling all the way back to the house. Her head rests against the window, and her eyes have fluttered closed. She's drunk. I can't remember the last time I got drunk. My system built up a tolerance to alcohol quickly since my father fed it to me so young. At first I hated how the alcohol made me feel—I had no control. The world would spin, and each time, I threw up. As I grew, my body adjusted to it. My father moved me on from beer to spirits. The transition to spirits was harder the next day. My hangovers would be killers.

Gail's neon open sign is off, and if I didn't have Mila, I would be in there demanding answers. I need to get Mila home first, then I can return here. There's no other reason for Gail to try to have me killed, only Dimitri, but Gail has been around the block a few times, so I never pictured her getting attached. She's a very clever business woman, or maybe I gave her way more credit than she was due.

Once I pull into the garage, I turn off the engine. Mila is still asleep. Her breath fogs up the window, and I have a moment of sitting here with her, in this odd sense of stillness. I'm very aware that no one has ever fallen asleep in my car before. No one would get comfortable enough, not with The Collector, and most certainly not in the trunk.

She doesn't stir as I lift her from the passenger seat and carry her into the sitting room. I know I need to cuff her to the radiator, but right now she needs some proper rest. I lay her on the couch and cover her small frame with a blanket. She's beautiful. I brush hair off her face and lean in to press a kiss to her lips. The taste of vodka is strong. She stirs and I leave her before I wake her up. She should sleep for a while.

I lock the sitting room door behind me before leaving the house. I know finding Gail now is wiser than waiting until later. She would expect me later, and when her men don't return, I have no doubt she will send more after me. But for now, Mila is safe. Safe from Gail, but not safe from Oleg or Victor.

The city approaches fast, and I pull up in the alleyway alongside Gail's. I check my gun before pushing it into the waistband of my trousers and getting out of the car. Boxes from a recent delivery, pallets, and two large metal bins line the far wall. I keep walking until the brick structure lowers to my height.

I scale the wall and jump the black iron gate. The round knob rotates in my fingers, but the door doesn't open. I expected it to be locked. I knock three times, then twice and three more, with a final single knock. It's a secret knock that's given to the heavy hitters who don't want to use the front door. I don't have to wait long until the door opens.

I push my way through and remove my gun. The security man raises his hands. I recognize the scar that runs down the left side of his face; he's been here for a while with Gail.

"Where is she?" I ask.

He shakes his head, pushing his hands higher into the air.

"Where is Gail?" I hold the gun closer to his face.

"She isn't here."

My gun connects with the side of his head, and his large form hits the ground hard. I step over the lump and move slowly through the empty club, discovering that he isn't lying—Gail isn't here. Her office is locked. It takes three kicks before the door gives way under my foot.

Gail is a smart woman. Anything of importance wouldn't be kept in here. It doesn't stop me from searching her office, though. I make a mess to let her know that I was here and I will be back.

Leaving through the front door, my phone bleeps with another collection. Brian Ledwidge is my next target. I don't like that he lives nearly an hour's drive away from me. I can't leave Mila alone, but bringing her on a job would be madness.

The car hums to life as I get in and reverse out of the alleyway. I slow down as I pass Gail's. It's still in darkness as I drive past. I pull up outside the club and read the address again for my next collection. Making a snap decision, I return to the house.

Mila is sitting when I enter the sitting room. Her head snaps up, and her gaze clashes with mine. Dark circles under her eyes have me second-guessing my decision, but leaving her here alone isn't wise. I hold a finger over my lips and beckon her forward. She doesn't move immediately, which surprises me, but she finally gets off the couch and follows me into the kitchen.

"We have to go out." I grab my wallet and the handcuffs. Mila rubs her eyes while glancing around the kitchen. Her gaze dances across everything except me.

"Where?"

"Just out, Mila." Using her name has the desired effect. She glances at me.

She looks to the handcuffs in my hands as she follows me out of the kitchen and into the garage. I slide into the car and wait as Mila hesitantly walks around to the passenger side and gets in. The minute she's inside, she starts to buckle her seat belt. I wait until she stops fidgeting.

"Show me your hands." The moment I say it, her hands tighten across her chest.

Her gaze darts to the handcuffs again. "Why? I'm not going any-where."

"Then give me your hands."

She glances away but relaxes her arms. I take a hand in mine. Hers are so small, and I think of how they felt on me. My cock twitches as I gently clamp the cuffs around her wrist. The click of the cuff causes her to look at me. Her eyes are wider, and I wonder if she's thinking the same thing I am. I'm picturing her cuffed to my bed upstairs. Her eyelids flutter closed, cutting me off. I lean over her, and her breath brushes my neck as I wrap the chain of the cuff through the bar on the door before securing it to her other wrist. The click of the cuff is my cue to sit back, but her quickening breaths have me glancing into her gaze. The smell of vodka fans across my face, and fear burns in her eyes. I want to reassure her, tell her I won't hurt her, but I can't make a promise like that. I quickly sit back and reverse out of the garage.

"Where are we going?" Mila's voice is small and tired as she stares out the window. The city moves past us, and I run a hand across my face to keep myself awake.

"I have a job to do," I answer.

Her head snaps up. "You're taking me on a collection?" Disbelief coats her words.

"I can't exactly leave you in the house, now, can I?" My voice is rough, and I take a quick peek at Mila to see her sink back into the chair. "More men will come," I say, gentler this time.

"Who sent them?" The curiosity in her voice isn't lost on me.

I glance at her and her eyes clash with mine. Too much information isn't wise, but who will she tell, and what difference will telling her make? None.

"Gail. You met her."

I take another quick peek at Mila. She's still watching me and her jaw is tighter. She appears more alert.

"The woman who stopped you on the street." Mila's words have a bite to them. She's leaning closer to me, but the handcuffs restrict her. She glances down at them in annoyance.

"Why?"

"That's the question I've been asking myself, too."

CHAPTER EIGHTEEN

MILA

I RATTLE THE HANDCUFFS again, and Nicholai's jaw tightens. I'm exhausted and have witnessed enough death for one day. He's still staring at me, and I can't stop the smile that grows slowly across my face.

"What are you smiling for?" His brows drag down.

My gaze flickers across all the tattoos that travel up his neck. My heart bounces in my chest, and my smile slowly melts away. My brain is tired. Maybe that's why I've become honest with him.

"Eric. He would die if he got to meet you."

Nicholai doesn't react. I don't expect him to. He doesn't know who Eric is. It has no meaning to him.

I'm smiling again, thinking of Eric. He was so much fun. I glance down at my nails. *He left you, Mila. Don't forget that.*

When I glance back at Nicholai, he's still watching me.

"I was sent to the mill as punishment by my father. I stole a car with my friend, Eric."

Surprise filters through Nicholai's eyes before his eyes grow darker. "You got sent to the mill as punishment."

It's not a question; it's an angry declaration.

"Yeah, it wasn't the first time I was caught acting out, but it was the final straw. I didn't have to work in the mill, though." Now it's my turn to glance away from Nicholai, and I'm wondering why I'm telling him all this. "I thought I would be locked up for a day or two, you know? To frighten me. He said you would come."

I glance back at Nicholai. "I was excited that I would meet you. I could tell Eric I actually got to meet The Collector." I swallow. "You never came."

My face is itchy, and I raise my hands to scratch it, only to have my movements restricted by the cuffs. I glance up at Nicholai again. I want him to say something, but his gaze bounces around my face. He frowns and my stomach dips.

"Who's your father?"

My heart pounds harder. "Oleg will come back for me," I say, and the stupid pleading in my voice doesn't go unnoticed. Nicholai has no power with these men, and my time is running out.

"Let me go," I whisper and chew my lip.

"Is Oleg your father?" Nicholai faces me, his tattooed hands joined in front of him.

I shake my head. "No, he's not."

He's waiting and I realize it doesn't matter anymore. For the first time, telling him who my father is won't matter. He could let me go or deliver me.

"Victor," I say, with an enormous amount of anger. I always hated him, even as a child. But I will never forgive him for the year in the mill. It changed me, twisted the innocence inside me and made me afraid of the world.

"Victor is your father," Nicholai repeats.

"Please, if you let me go…"

"Stop!" Nicholai's roar has my lips clamping together. He glares at me, and I sink into the seat.

"Your name is Milagros."

Hearing my full name makes me shudder. "Yes."

I don't know what to think when Nicholai climbs out of the car. The slam of the door has me jumping slightly. It doesn't matter who I am. I know the lie the moment it leaves my lips. But I am under no obligation to tell him who I am. I try to push the guilt aside as Nicholai leaves through a side door into a building. The moment he disappears, I start to yank on the cuffs. Stretching as far as I can, I attempt to reach the glove compartment to no avail. A door slams. That was quick. The moment I glance up, I frown as a man rushes toward the car. I yank the cuffs as he climbs in.

"What are you doing?" Panic tears through me as he scrambles for the keys Nicholai left in the ignition.

"What are you doing?" I scream as the engine starts, and we're reversing down the side road. My gaze clashes with Nicholai's as he bursts from the side door. Blood flows down the side of his face. The driver curses as he spins the car, and we nearly hit oncoming traffic. I'm screaming as I try to make myself smaller.

His foot hits the pedal, and we're speeding.

"Stop the car! Let me out!"

He glances at me for the first time. His gaze flickers to the cuffs. "Why are you cuffed in The Collector's car?"

"Are you a collector too?" I ask.

He nods and tightens his jaw before facing forward. He doesn't appear to be a criminal. He looks like a man who might work in a bank. His loose suit and fading hair speak of maybe kids, a wife, and a mortgage. I clock the ring on his finger. Yep, he's married.

"Please." I soften my voice. "If you let me out, I might have a chance."

He glances at me again. "No. Maybe I can use you as a bargaining chip."

I snort and stare out the window. "Good luck with that."

My body tenses as he swerves to the left, sending me sailing into the door. My wrist burns.

"Fuck!"

I try to turn in my seat to see what has him so panicked.

"He found us."

"Of course he did. He's The Collector."

How did I ever think I could outrun him? The man grows too frantic and is swerving in and out of traffic. He's going to get us killed.

"You need to calm down and get out of the city," I tell him.

"Listen to me, lady—I don't need driving lessons from you. So sit back and stay quiet." Sweat soaks the side of his face. I have no choice but to sit back as he drives like a lunatic.

"We are so easy to spot," I try to tell him again. If he relaxes, we might blend better.

"Shut your mouth." His words are hushed as he grips the steering wheel.

I don't know how we do it, but we leave the city and make it out to the countryside. I can't stop the laugh that bubbles up my throat.

"What are you laughing at?" He sounds calmer now.

"Nothing." I glare out the window. The irony that he's driving toward the can isn't lost on me, but I'm not sharing that information with him.

"So what did you do?" he asks me.

"I stole a car. What did you do?" I glance at him as he pulls his tie off.

"I'm innocent."

His eyes meet mine. "What? You don't believe me?"

"It doesn't matter if I believe..." My words are cut off as a car slams into the driver's side, sending us off the road. Dust kicks up, leaving us completely blind. I glance at the driver, who struggles to control the car.

I close my eyes and send a prayer up to God to let me walk away from this. I don't want to die in a car. I don't think my survival would be likely while handcuffed to the door. A scream is ripped from my throat as metal collides with metal. I want to scream and tell him to get back on the road so we can have some visibility. He's spinning the wheel in fear of what he can't see. This time, the impact is jarring. The collision races through my bones, and I curl myself up as the car spins out of control. There's a moment where I think, *Is this really it? Is this how I leave the world?* It's a devastating thought. The worst part is, I'm not ready to leave yet. I'm not ready to leave Nicholai. With that final disturbing thought, we come to an abrupt stop.

The blood roars in my ears as I open my eyes and scan my body. I seem to be in one piece. I glance at the driver. He's stunned. The door opens and he hasn't a second before he's dragged out into the dust-filled air. I can't see anything.

The dust lights up twice as Nicholai fires a gun. My heart threatens to rip from my chest. What if the man was carrying a gun? What if Nicholai is injured? The man already got a hit on him. The dust moves as a shape walks to the car. I push back into the door.

Nicholai climbs in, his gaze dancing across my flesh, and when his eyes meet mine, they swim with relief. He doesn't speak as he reaches across and uncuffs my hands. My wrists are red and bleeding lightly in three places. But I'm alive. I don't think but react, and I'm hugging Nicholai. He doesn't hug me back and still I cling to him anyway as my throat burns. The emotion is a double-edged sword. Seeing him means I'm alive, but it also means the end will come soon and I will be handed over.

Nicholai pushes me back slowly, and my gaze moves to the body on the ground outside the driver's door. The dust has almost settled, and I can see the man with two bullet holes in his head. Blood oozes from the wound.

"Don't you ever get sick of it?" I can't look away from the man. His finger clad in the silver band has my stomach hollowing out.

"Not until now." His soft words have me looking at him. His dark eyes would bring anyone to their knees, and I am falling hard.

Love
Ali

CHAPTER NINETEEN

NICHOLAI

I'M STARING INTO BLUE eyes. I'm staring into the eyes of Victor's daughter. The implications just multiplied. I knew she was different, even important, but she is my boss's daughter. I've never seen Victor or his family, but their names are familiar to me. I never thought I would be collecting his daughter, never mind keeping her in my home.

"It doesn't make sense." She's rubbing her wrists, blood dragging across her skin. What price would we pay for hurting her?

"Why would Oleg put his hands on you?" I don't understand that. Touching Victor's family would be a death sentence.

"He's my father's right-hand man."

That information surprises me. I knew he's high up, but I didn't know he's that high up. "Does your father know he's hitting you?"

Mila glances away from me, and I reach out and grip her face gently.

She frowns and shakes her head. "My father locked me up in the mill, Nicholai."

I release her. That's a large pill to swallow. The dust has settled outside. I need to get the body into the trunk and get out of here.

"We can't go back to the house." I climb out of the car but pause and glance back in at Mila. "Who's Eric?"

"My friend. Well, he was once my friend." Pain radiates in her blue eyes.

I drag Brian to the back of my car. After popping the trunk, I lift him in. The driver side is painful to glance at; the damage is colossal. The car will have to be replaced. I climb back in and it takes three attempts to close the driver door. I keep glancing at Mila. I have no idea what to do with her.

"You should tell your father that Oleg hit you."

Her head snaps up to me. "What? When you leave me at the can?"

I face forward and grip the steering wheel. When I got the message, I couldn't defy him.

"He's your father. He won't hurt you."

Her snort has me peeking at her again. "Yeah, I'm going to return to hugs and picnics."

My temper sparks, and I tighten my hands on the steering wheel as I bring the car back onto the road.

The rest of the drive to the can is silent. I throw Brian's body in, and it takes me a few minutes to close the door. I'm tired. I'm tired of collecting for faces I never see, for reasons I don't know.

Mila's lids rest on her cheeks, but she isn't asleep. I can tell from the rise and fall of her chest. "We can't go home."

She sits up. "What happens when Oleg arrives and I'm not there?"

"You said you witnessed him killing a girl."

She flinches like I struck her but nods. "Yeah."

"With that knowledge, you could use it against him."

"No one would believe me, Nicholai."

I start the car again. "If that was true, then Oleg wouldn't be trying to frighten you to keep you quiet."

The next time I see him, I'll struggle not to take his pitiful life. I exhale loudly to try to keep the darkness at bay.

I park at the furthest corner of the car park of the motel. "I'll get us checked in."

Mila's eyes widen like she can't believe I'm leaving her. The chip I had placed in her neck allowed me to find her and Brian easily. Not that it was hard with his erratic driving, but it showed me where they were, which is how I found them.

"Don't try to run." My threat falls flat. Nerves squirm in my stomach as I leave the car. Leaving her alone now feels unnatural. I glance back at the car the moment I reach the front door of the reception. She's still sitting in the car. I enter and order a room. The receptionist doesn't ask questions, just takes the payment.

I hide my surprise as I return to the car to see Mila staring out the passenger window. Her gaze flicks up to mine as I open her door.

"Come on." After she climbs out, I reach in and pick the hand-cuffs off the ground. I hope I don't have to use them.

The motel room is clean, and I immediately draw the curtains. "You need to get some rest." Mila looks exhausted.

I turn to an empty room. My hand immediately goes for the gun in my waistband. It's a reflex, but I pause as Mila steps back into the room with a first aid kit in her hands.

"Sit down." She swallows before dropping my gaze.

I take my fingers off the gun and pull off my suit jacket before sitting on the bed. The bed dips as she sits down beside me. Her hands move quickly across the bandages until they land on disin-fectant wipes.

Her blue eyes jump to me, and I want to kiss her. She's stunning.

"Why are you smiling?"

"The moment you got into the passenger side of my car, I knew you were different." I reach out, and she doesn't move away from my touch. She might not understand what I'm saying, but I lean my forehead against hers and inhale her scent.

"What have you gotten me into?" I ask her.

The pulse flickers in her neck. I place a kiss on her jawline, and her muscles tense.

Small hands push against my chest. "Let me clean your face."

I sit back and let her take care of me, closing my eyes as she runs the wipe across the cut. I had been stunned by the news that she's Victor's daughter. Brian caught me off guard. No one had ever caught me off guard before. Mila seems to have the ability to jumble my senses.

"Are you okay?" Her voice is soft, and I open my eyes.

"Yeah, it was a lapse in judgment."

Her smirk has me smiling. She presses a Band-Aid against the cut and the pain races down the side of my face, but I don't look away from her.

"Let me see your wrists." They aren't bad; I just want an excuse to touch her.

But she stands up, gathering the medical supplies and placing them back into the box. "I'm fine. I just need a shower."

Thoughts of her in the shower have my trousers tightening. I don't say anything as she leaves and closes the door to the bathroom behind her. I get up and check the window again. It's still dark. We need to sleep.

After fixing the curtains, I pull off my tie and open the top button of my shirt before kicking off my shoes. The red dot that shows where Mila is blinks. It's a habit now to check on her. She's in the shower.

I drop the phone on the bed, then remove my trousers and pull off my shirt. My body aches from the car chase and exhaustion. I can't think clearly, and going back to the house with the threat of Gail hanging over us isn't wise. I need rest before we can return. Otherwise, I couldn't possibly protect Mila. The sheets are clean as I pull back the duvet and get in. I close my eyes and listen as the water stops running. I'm picturing her soft body. I'm remembering how it felt to have my cock buried inside her. She's perfection.

The door to the bathroom opens, and I keep my eyes closed. She doesn't move, and I'm tempted to peek. A few breaths later, she's moving around the room. I slowly open my eyes as she opens drawers and closes them one after another.

"What are you looking for?"

"A hair dryer." She speaks over her shoulder. Her small hands hold the towel tight against her chest.

She swings around and marches to the bedside table beside me. Bending over, she opens the drawer. "How can a motel room not have a hair dryer?"

She looks like a shampoo commercial with her long blonde hair flowing down her back. Her gaze meets mine, and I love the pink hue that burns her cheeks. I sit up in the bed, and her gaze travels across me. She sucks in her bottom lip and my cock twitches. I reach up for her and pull her down. She comes with no resistance at all. She doesn't let the towel go as she climbs onto the bed. Her lips are cold and soft. I run my tongue along them and she shivers. One hand touches my shoulders, and I use the opportunity to remove the towel from her body.

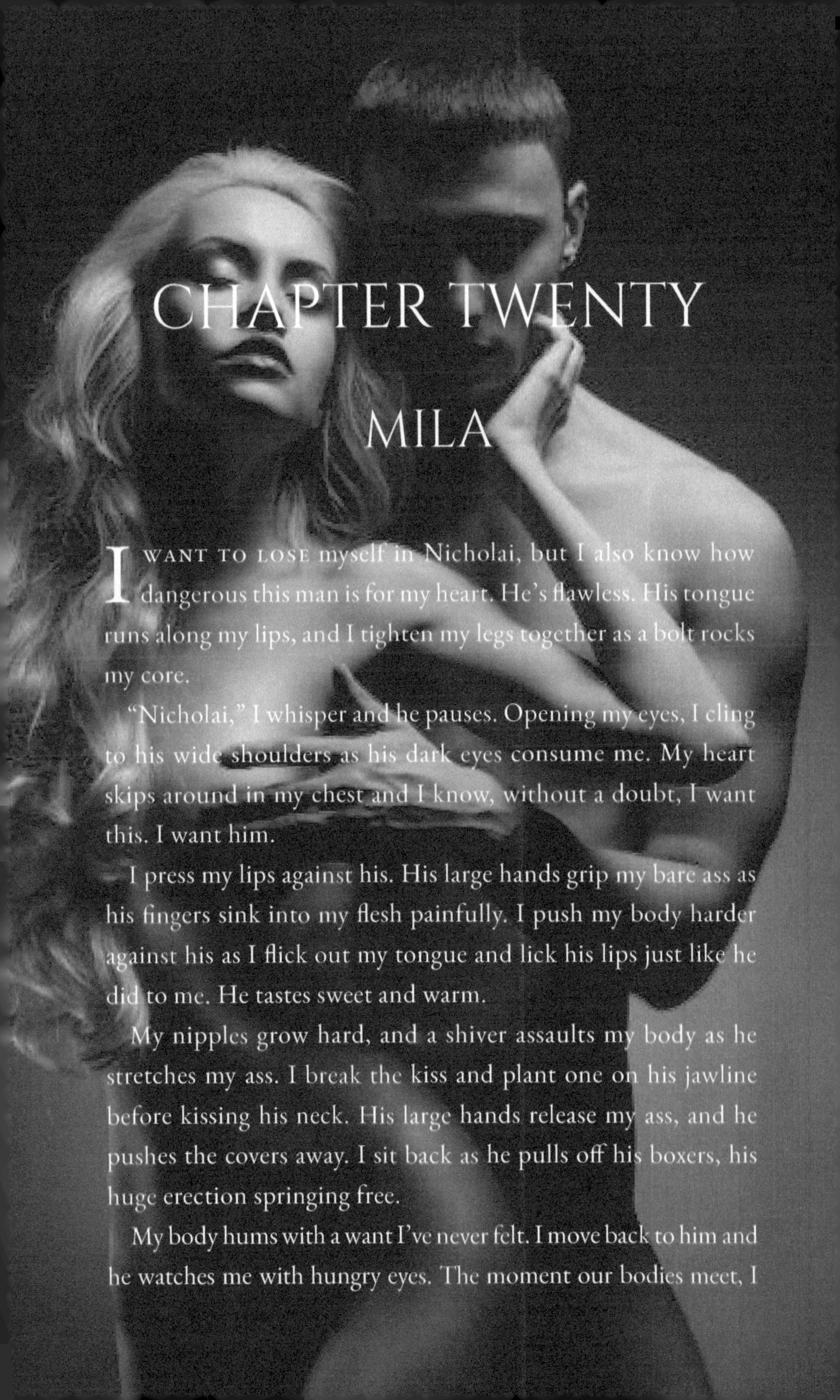

CHAPTER TWENTY

MILA

I WANT TO LOSE myself in Nicholai, but I also know how dangerous this man is for my heart. He's flawless. His tongue runs along my lips, and I tighten my legs together as a bolt rocks my core.

"Nicholai," I whisper and he pauses. Opening my eyes, I cling to his wide shoulders as his dark eyes consume me. My heart skips around in my chest and I know, without a doubt, I want this. I want him.

I press my lips against his. His large hands grip my bare ass as his fingers sink into my flesh painfully. I push my body harder against his as I flick out my tongue and lick his lips just like he did to me. He tastes sweet and warm.

My nipples grow hard, and a shiver assaults my body as he stretches my ass. I break the kiss and plant one on his jawline before kissing his neck. His large hands release my ass, and he pushes the covers away. I sit back as he pulls off his boxers, his huge erection springing free.

My body hums with a want I've never felt. I move back to him and he watches me with hungry eyes. The moment our bodies meet, I want him inside me. His hands grip my ass again, and I want them on my pussy—I want them inside. I want him to fill me.

Our lips clash and I run my hand down his body, taking his huge cock in my hand. He falls closer and groans into my ear. My core tightens and I can feel the wetness on the inside of my thigh. His hand leaves my ass and returns a moment later with some of the wetness from my thigh. I freeze as he rubs warm liquid onto my asshole. The surprise wears off, and I stroke his cock again. He groans and dips a finger into my ass. All the nerves have me arching my back out, wanting him deeper inside me. He does, and I stroke his cock harder, the tip hitting my stomach. His other hand holds my ass stretched, and he pushes two fingers in. I cry out at the sensation, not sure if I want him to stop or to keep going. I yank his cock and move faster.

"Turn around for me, Mila."

His words are breathy, and I release his cock. His fingers slowly leave my ass, and I feel the loss immediately. I turn around. Nicholai pushes down on the base of my back until I'm on all fours with my ass cocked in the air. I'm soaking just thinking of him fucking me.

"Has anyone fucked your ass before?" he asks.

Liquid touches my asshole, and I clench before relaxing. His fingers circle and stroke before dipping in.

"No." I close my eyes and he buries his finger inside me. When his other hand touches my pussy, I'm ready to lose it. Every nerve ending is on fire.

He pushes a second finger into my ass before slipping them out. His fingers leave my pussy, and my eyes spring open as his cock enters my ass. I feel stretched, and the pain is short-lived as he eases in.

"You're perfect." He pushes deeper, and I push back into him, wanting more and more. He starts to fuck my ass harder, and I can't stop the cries that fall from my lips. Nicholai groans too as he pounds my ass, his balls slapping against my pussy as I call his name, wanting more, wanting to come. It's all too much.

He removes his cock from my ass, and I want to see what he's doing, but he enters again, this time fast and hard. The impact has me crying out as he continues to slam into my ass, dragging my body up until my back is flush with his chest. Nicholai grips my neck as he fucks my ass hard and fast. I'm screaming and squirming. His hand encases my breast and he pinches my nipple.

His quick movements slam into my ass, and I can't hold off any longer. He rolls my nipple between his forefinger and thumb while his other hand tightens around my throat. His cock fills me and I come. The liquid pours down my thigh as he continues to fuck me with a savagery that has him pouring his seed inside my ass.

Nicholai loosens his hold on my neck and slowly pulls out of me. I don't move as his chest rises and falls against my back. I close my eyes and enjoy the sound of our raspy breaths that mingle together. His hot breath touches my sweaty neck before he places a kiss on my shoulder. I smile with my eyes closed as he presses another kiss to the back of my neck before kissing my other shoulder.

My stomach flips and erupts with butterflies at the tenderness of the kisses. I glance down as large tattooed hands wrap around my waist. I'm staring at them, wondering how something so dangerous looking could be so gentle. I cover his hands with mine. Exhaustion tugs at me, and all the energy is zapped from my body.

I let Nicholai's hands go, and he unwinds them from me. I glance at him over my shoulder, and my stomach squirms when I meet his dark eyes. I don't say all I want to say. Instead, I shuffle off the bed and enter the shower for the second time tonight. I don't feel violated like I thought I would. I saw Oleg do the same thing to Liddi, but it looked painful and rough. I couldn't understand any pleasure coming from it, but it is powerful. Nicholai is powerful.

He's looking at his phone when I enter the bedroom. His gaze snaps up to mine and he stands up, still fully naked. He's a beast of a man, and I still can't take him all in as he moves closer. He pauses and bends his six-foot frame, placing a kiss on my cheek.

"I'm going for a shower."

I nod. "Okay."

When I glance up, he's watching me. I know this thing between us is dangerous and scary, but I don't want it to end. I climb into the bed wrapped in the motel's towel, and that's how I fall asleep.

CHAPTER TWENTY ONE

NICHOLAI

She's asleep when I return to the room. Her chest rises and falls in a soft rhythm. I sit on the edge of the bed and lean in, pushing blonde hair off her face. She's perfect.

She's Victor's daughter, I remind myself. I'm here to collect her. I've been checking my phone, waiting for the message to come in, to deliver her to the can. I already know the answer to the message. I won't do it. I can't give her up. But I don't know how to keep her. Oleg is a huge problem... or he could end up being part of the solution. I place a kiss on her cheek, and I hear the one word echo through my mind that seemed to be there from the start.

Mine.

She is mine, not Victor's. I touch her face again. What did she see at the mill? What kind of man places his daughter in a dungeon like that? The most ruthless leader of them all. The leader of the Bratva. That would have caused shock waves through the Bratva.

Why hadn't I heard about it? I try to jog my memory, but I have no recollection of it.

I'm ready to get up when my phone beeps from the bedside table. I'm staring at it like it might reveal who it is before I walk around and pick it up.

It's a message from Gail to meet her at the club. She got my little message. Leaving Mila here is far safer than taking her with me.

I get dressed and feel uneasy leaving Mila like this. I have the chip in her neck to track her, but I don't want to have to track her. I place a handcuff as carefully as possible around her wrist and click it closed. She stirs slightly as I fasten the other one through the bar of the bed. It isn't ideal, but it will have to do for now. I take one final look at her before leaving and making my way to Gail's.

I sit outside, my instincts, which have kept me alive this long, keeping me in the car. It's all too easy. Her showing up here doesn't make sense. Or, I could be getting paranoid. She sent men, and each time they didn't arrive back. Maybe she's given up trying to kill me, or maybe this is an ambush.

I ring her number, and she answers on the second ring.

"Turn on the neon sign," I say into the phone.

"What?" She sounds alarmed. She's moving quickly.

"I'm waiting, Gail." I know she should have reached the switches by now.

"Turn it on," I repeat.

"It's not working." Her lie is swallowed so easily.

"What's waiting inside the club?" I ask. "Or should I say how many?"

"You killed Dimitri."

"I collected Dimitri. He ran. There is a clear difference."

"He's dead. That's all I know." She's angry.

"This is why women will never rule. You're too emotional."

"You know you left my daughter fatherless."

Guilt churns in my stomach for the first time. He told me he had a daughter. I swallow that bit of information and tighten my hold on any guilt I feel.

"I leave a lot of daughters and sons fatherless. It's my job. You know what I do. You know what I am."

"My men—where are they?" Her voice is more controlled now. If I didn't know better, I'd think she didn't really care that much for Dimitri, that he's just a smoke screen.

"Dead. Every one of them." She knew that already. I check the front of the club. She's stalling me again. I turn the engine on and pull away from the curb of the club. As I drive past, I see several men making their way along the wall. The first one runs out onto the street as I move past.

"I will find out where you live and end your life." I speak clearly as I glance in the rearview mirror.

"You've pissed off some very powerful people, Nicholai. I like you. So there is your warning."

I laugh at the arrogance. "Warning?"

"I hear you have precious cargo." My heart pounds heavier, and my stomach sours as I think of Mila back at the motel. I push my foot harder to the floor. Did I make a mistake leaving her alone? Or am I being followed? I quickly bring up the tracking app. She's still at the motel, and the dot is blinking in one spot. I'm hoping that means she's asleep.

"You need to be more comprehensive about what precious cargo means." I want to keep her on the phone, but Gail isn't stupid.

"Goodbye, Nicholai." She hangs up, and I curse her as I speed back to the motel. We need to move. They could be following me.

The moment I burst through the door, Mila screams and tries to scramble off the bed, only to be dragged back by the cuffs.

"What the hell?" She's yanking on them.

"Get dressed." I take the cuffs and remove them from her wrists. She doesn't move.

"Now, Mila!" I'm shouting, and I stop and take a calming breath. Turning to Mila, I kneel down in front of her.

"I think they know we're here, so we need to leave."

"Why are you helping me?" The question is so heavy, and I honestly don't know how to answer it, so I don't. Instead, I stand and can't help but run my hand along her soft skin.

"Please, get dressed."

She gets up and silently puts on her clothes. All I can think of as I stare at her is that I can't lose her. And this is why I should never let anyone get close. It's dangerous. Mila is dangerous.

I keep checking the rearview mirror, but we aren't being followed. "Get some rest," I tell Mila as the sun rises.

"I got some sleep. Why don't you sleep and I'll drive?" I'm ready to laugh, but I'm exhausted and not sure how long I'll be able to stay awake. I pull over and get out of the driver's side. Mila climbs across, and she's grinning when I climb into the passenger seat while readjusting the seat.

"I'm driving The Collectors car," she sings. The childlike excitement in her eyes leaves as I quickly tighten the cuff around her wrist.

"What?"

I tighten the other one to my wrist. "Can't have you pulling over and running when I fall asleep."

She pulls my arm, and I try to pretend it isn't painful.

"How the hell can I drive like this?" She yanks my arm again, and I pull her as I close the door. Her cheeks grow red with anger, and I suppress the smile that tugs at my lips.

Lying back, I close my eyes as she starts the car. My arm is yanked every two seconds, and I lean more toward Mila, until my arm is nearly on her lap. I like the heat of her skin under my fingertips, and that's how I fall asleep, with the smell of Mila and the warmth of her leg pouring into the tips of my fingers. They skitter across her skin every few moments until my mind drags me into a dark sleep.

My arm is pulled again.

"Nicholai."

I'm alert at the urgency in Mila's voice.

"We're being followed."

I sit up straighter, and she pulls my arm back toward the steering wheel. The visor has a small mirror I look through as I take the key out of my pocket. A red sedan is behind us.

"How long has it been following us?" I uncuff our hands.

"I'm not sure. I've only noticed it the last two turns, but I have no idea how long it's been following us."

"Take a left off this road," I say, and watch as we slip off the road. The red sedan doesn't follow, but I make Mila take several lefts and rights. The car would attract attention in its condition.

We pass a sign that says *23 kilometers to High Park*.

"Keep going straight." I take out my phone as a message from my gate at home is telling me I have two visitors. I pull up the footage and pause when Oleg's face fills the camera. He drives off. The second car has tinted windows. No one gets out, but it pauses for a moment before driving off. I close the phone and glance at Mila. She looks tired. We need to rest.

I continue to give her directions until we come to a set of large green gates. "When we go in here, you're my girlfriend. We had a rough night. That's it."

I glance at Mila. Her fingers tighten around the steering wheel. She turns to me. "Okay." Her voice is small.

The part I need to tell her is that if she knew who I was, then she would have heard of The Handler. I look back at the gates. I have nowhere else to take Mila. My car is identifiable. I have no cash, only a card they can trace.

"Have you heard of The Handler?"

Mila's eyes grow wide, confirming she has. "Is this his house?" She ducks down over the steering wheel, looking up at the mini castle.

"Yes. He might help us."

Mila's attention returns to me. "Might?" She's suppressing a smile.

"This isn't a joke."

Her smile slips. "I'm sorry. I've heard of The Handler, but to think I'm going to meet him is exciting."

"Girls don't normally get excited over our titles." In fact, they run the other way.

"I grew up with Eric, and he never shut up about all the high hitters, so it rubbed off." She shrugs. "I suppose."

Eric. That boy's name again. I don't like it.

"Just let me do the talking. And remember, you're my girlfriend."

Her cheeks pinken and she tucks a strand of blonde hair behind her ear.

"We better swap." I get out and walk to the driver's side as she climbs into the passenger. I pull up closer to the gates and hit the bell. I know there are cameras everywhere. The Handler is Bratva's personal hit man. He needs to be protected at all times. It's been years since we saw each other.

The gates pull open, and I glance at Mila. "Don't say who you are," I tell her before driving up the drive.

"Who my father is?" she says, staring out the window.

"Yeah."

I don't think anyone knows what Victor's daughter looks like. I hadn't known, and right now, I hang onto that as we pull up outside Lucca's house. The front door opens, and two large men step aside as Lucca jogs down the steps. His arms are wide and he's wearing a grin.

"Oh my God," Mila whispers, and I'm tempted to look at her, but instead I climb out.

"Nic." Lucca embraces me, and I pat his back heavily.

"Lucca."

He pushes the sunglasses onto the top of his head. Silver eyes take in my car. "What the fuck happened?"

His eyes skip across all the damage and to Mila, who steps out of the car. My stomach tightens, and I try not to flinch as she moves around the car.

"Lucca, this is my girlfriend, Mila."

Lucca turns to me. "Girlfriend?"

I get the question. In our line of work, you don't get attached. He nods his head, and his sunglasses fall back down on his face.

"Hi." Mila speaks softly, and I hate the awe I see in her eyes as she looks up at Lucca. He towers over her at six feet seven inches—he's a big guy. In prison, no one fucked with him, and anyone that did was found hanging in their cells the next day.

The blue silk shirt billows out as he jogs up the steps of his house. His security moves back and lets us in.

"So great to see you." He takes off the glasses once we enter. His dark hair is slicked back. I remember it being longer when we did time together.

"I need a place to hunker," I tell him.

Lucca moves up to me. "My home is your home."

I grip his forearm. "Thanks, brother."

This is what we do. We have each other's back when we need it. I never thought I would need anyone, but I also never thought someone would need me. I turn to Mila, who's watching us.

"You want a drink, sweetheart?" Lucca talks loudly to Mila, like she can't hear him. Women always flock around him, but if they aren't on top of him, he doesn't have much time for them.

"No, thank you." Mila frowns before glancing at me.

"She can hear you, Lucca," I sneer.

He slaps my forearm.

"Let's have a drink." His gaze flickers to Mila. It's like he's trying to tell me to lose the tail.

Lucca claps his hands loudly, and a tall brunette wearing a leopard print dress appears in the doorway.

"I'm not a dog, Luc." The brunette slams a hand on her hips. She has no fear of Lucca. Has he settled down too?

"Anita, this is Mila. Can you show her to a room and give her some clothes? You know, make her feel welcome."

Anita's silver eyes roam my frame before she turns to Mila.

"Let me show you around, kitten."

Mila's gaze jumps to me, and I nod at her. She forces a smile at Anita and they leave.

"She's my sister." Lucca fills in the blank as I follow him out of the hallway.

Now he'll want to know why I'm here. I'm not sure how much I want to tell him.

CHAPTER TWENTY TWO

MILA

"**S**ize six?" Anita's gaze scans me from the top of my head to the tips of my toes.

"Yeah." Her long legs go on forever. I don't like how she looked at Nicholai.

She's sizing me up, so I don't shy away, and I do the same to her. Is this who is dating The Handler?

We both have questions, but I remember what Nicholai told me about him doing most of the talking. These people might be helping us, but I have to remember that they're still dangerous people.

Anita opens a door into a large room with a four-poster bed. My gaze immediately moves to the ceiling. No mirror. The room is beautifully decorated with high quality and dark furnishings.

"You can stay in this room." She pushes open a door that leads into a bathroom. "Bathroom," she tells me and smiles.

"I'll get you some clothes, kitten."

I don't like the endearment, but I force a smile. "Thank you."

Once she leaves, I enter the bathroom. A large bath that could hold a few people dominates the room.

Anita returns and I enter the bedroom. She places the clothes on a trunk at the base of the bed.

"Anything else I can get you, kitten?" She's smiling sweetly, but all my senses are telling me this woman is dangerous.

"No, thanks. I might just get some rest. "

She doesn't leave immediately, and I force a smile. "Thanks, once again."

She finally leaves me alone, and I lie down on the bed. My mind decides to conjure the image of the man's hand clad in a silver band. Two bullet holes in his forehead have me tightening my eyes. Is someone waiting for him at home?

I sit up and rub my eyes, trying to push the image away. A shiver assaults my body, and I have no idea if it's the cold or the idea of being surrounded by unfamiliar things. I want Nicholai here with me. I want to lie in his arms and fall asleep. My stomach twists when I picture him. I miss him. Frowning, I get up off the bed. I shouldn't miss a man like The Collector. I think I have gone beyond pretending that I don't have feelings for Nicholai. I'm falling for him hard and fast.

My cheeks burn. What kind of person does that make me? To fall for someone who just kills on a whim? Who takes husbands from wives? I grew up in the middle of the Bratva, but I didn't see the violence. I heard the stories from Eric, but to me, it was just that—stories. It wasn't until I entered the mill that the horror of what we were really came true.

I leave the bedroom and try to push my dark thoughts away as I run the shower and strip off, but they don't leave me. I'm back in that cell. Liddi's screams pierce me all the way down to my soul.

I should have stopped Oleg. I should have saved her. I was such a coward.

I escape the shower and towel myself off. I can't think. I don't want to. The clothes Anita left out for me are all tight. I sigh but pull on the black leggings and a red string top. They don't leave anything to the imagination, but they're clean.

I run my fingers through my hair before climbing into bed. I know I need sleep. My eyes burn with tiredness, but it's hard in a foreign place. I tell myself that Nicholai won't let any harm come to me. So far, he's kept me safe; he's running because of me. Or maybe that's what I've told myself, that Nicholai is running because of me. He could be running because of Gail. What did he do to her? Take someone she loved?

I sit up in the bed. Sleep won't come, and I don't want to be alone with my thoughts. Leaving the bedroom, my footsteps are silenced from the carpet that cushions my bare feet. I catch myself in a full-length mirror at the end of the hall. I tug the top away from me, but once I release the red fabric, it clings right back to my skin. Grabbing my blonde hair, I pull it over my shoulder. My bruises are fading fast. I look away from the mirror as I continue down the stairs. My gaze collides with Anita's.

"Thought I heard you moving, kitten."

"Where's Nicholai?" Calling him The Collector was on the tip of my tongue.

"My clothes look good on you."

I pull the top again. "They're a little tight."

Anita flashes me a smile. "They are this way." She flicks long curly locks behind her shoulder.

I feel small and childlike compared to Anita. She has curves, and any man would stop to look at her.

She opens a set of glass doors, and the steam from the pool room instantly touches my skin. A pool runs the full length of the room. Lucca is in it, and I can't stop staring at his body, which is just as heavily coated in tattoos as Nicholai's.

Nicholai sits on a chair close to the pool. He has removed his jacket and tie and opened the top two buttons of his shirt. His dark eyes zoom up to mine, and I pause in my stride as his gaze roams across my body. I continue to follow Anita, and Lucca watches me as closely as Nicholai does. Each step is nervous until I reach them. Now I have no idea what to say.

"I couldn't sleep," I blurt out to Nicholai and just focus on him and no one else.

His smile is soft, and he drags a chair over beside him. Relief swims through me at the invitation to sit beside him. I take it up quickly and drag my legs up into the chair. Lucca's gaze is heavy on me, but I keep my focus on Nicholai.

Nicholai startles me when he reaches across and wraps his hand around mine.

"Are you staying with us long?" Anita asks Nicholai, dragging everyone's attention to her.

"He can stay as long as he wants."

It's the first time I've heard a serious undertone to Lucca's voice. I watch him as he stares at Anita.

"I'm only asking," Anita retorts, and Lucca's gaze swings around to us, catching my eye.

"You can stay as long as you want." He's speaking to me, and I can feel my cheeks heat.

"Thank you, Lucca."

His smile lights up his silver eyes. "You're welcome, Mila." He grins at Nicholai before diving under the water and disappearing. He reappears at the end of the pool, pulls himself out of the water, and leaves the pool room.

My attention returns to Anita, who smiles at me before she turns and walks slowly along the pool. She sways her hips more now, and I glance at Nicholai, expecting him to be watching Anita. My heart beats fast as my gaze clashes with his dark eyes.

"Are you okay?" His concern has me smiling.

"I am now," I answer honestly, and he tightens his hand on mine.

CHAPTER TWENTY THREE

NICHOLAI

I WANT MILA OUT of the clothes she's wearing for more reasons than one. They leave nothing to the imagination. I don't want Lucca looking at her. I still haven't released her hand, and she's staring at our joined fingers.

"What are we doing here?" Her gaze jumps up to me. I hear the underlying question in her words. *What are we doing?*

"We'll stay awhile, until I can figure a few things out."

Her blue eyes jump to my lips before rising back up to meet my eyes. "Am I one of those things?"

"Yes." I don't want to discuss her situation. I don't have a solution, but I know I'm not giving her up. I have no idea how I can hold on to her, but I will try.

Her gaze bores into mine, and I release her hand and stand up.

She watches me as I pull off my shirt. I love how her eyes widen and drag down my chest. I open the belt of my trousers, and she's waiting.

"What are you doing?"

"Going for a swim." I kick off my trousers and pull down my boxers. I don't hide my erection, which has been growing harder the longer I'm around her.

She sucks in her bottom lip as I jump into the pool. The surface cracks open, and the lukewarm water encircles me as I swim the full length of the pool.

My ear picks up the disruption in the water, and I break the surface. My gaze dances to the seats Mila and I had occupied. On hers, her clothes are piled. My gaze searches for her, and when her blonde head breaks the surface, I swim slowly to her as she brushes water from her face. She's naked; her body shimmers under the water, and my erection grows harder.

"I thought a swim sounded nice." She smiles as I swim closer, and I mirror her smile.

"I'll admit, it is far nicer with you in it." I reach her. "Naked," I add.

She exhales loudly through her nose as I drag her body against mine. Her hands instantly wrap around my neck, and my cock brushes her stomach.

"I like you naked, too." She speaks without smiling. She leans out before pressing her lips against mine.

I move both of us to the side of the pool to help support me as I greedily take the kiss from her. She's perfect against my body, and I love that she's trapped as I slip my hand down and touch her clit. She breathes heavily against my lips, and I move my fingers until they touch her opening.

I push one in, and all I want to do is fuck her hard against the side of the pool. I keep moving my finger in and out before dragging it up to her clit. She squirms and whimpers between kisses as I keep my lips pressed against hers. Her hands tighten on my neck, and she pushes her body against mine, moving her legs up my thigh.

I remove my hand from her pussy and easily lift her so her legs wrap around me. I break the kiss, and her eyes swim as she stares up at me. I place my cock at her opening, then push it in. I exhale as her tight pussy wraps around me and I start to fuck her. Water sloshes up on the tiles the faster I move, but it's not fast enough, not deep enough. I want more of Mila. Her hands tighten around my neck as I continue to fuck her as fast and as hard as I can.

"I'm going to come," she whispers in my ear, and when she tenses around my cock, I relish in her release. I slow my pace down and stop fucking her. I want to empty myself in her so badly, but I'm aware we're in a pool. When I pull out of her, my cock throbs with need. It's almost painful. But I focus on Mila's beautiful flushed cheeks.

"Stay in the pool. I'll be back in a minute." I press a kiss to her plump lips before gripping the tiles behind her and pulling myself out of the pool. I enter a small room to the left. It's a toilet, but my cock demands relief. The moment I have the door closed, I take my shaft in my hand and start to pump. I'm picturing Mila up on all fours, her ass in the air. I'm imagining pounding my cock into her ass. I quicken my strokes but pause as the door opens.

Mila enters and closes the door softly behind her. She's wrapped in a towel as she falls to her knees. The moment my cock is in her mouth, I throw my head back. Her mouth is small, but she takes as much of me as she can. Her warm mouth moves quickly over my cock. I know it won't take much for me to come. When her hands cup and squeeze my balls, my precum squirts into her mouth. She tightens her lips and moves them faster over my cock until I come in her mouth. Her movements slow, and she looks up at me as she swallows my seed. Silently, she gets up and leaves the small room. I wait a moment before leaving too.

She's pulled her leggings back on and tugs the red top back on. Her gaze swings to me, and she smiles sweetly. When she steps up to me and presses a kiss against my lips, I'm ready to stop her. I normally wouldn't kiss any woman who just blew me off, but Mila's lips just turn me on again.

"You should put on some clothes." She smiles into the kiss.

"You don't like what you see?" I ask her, and she grins.

"I don't want anyone else seeing you." The moment she says the words, horror fills her blue eyes and she steps away from me.

"What's wrong?" I step toward her.

She holds her hands up. "Nothing." She tries to smile, but it doesn't reach her eyes.

I leave it and get dressed. I don't put my jacket or tie back on. "Lucca is having a few people over tonight, so we will be expected to join them. Even for a short while."

Mila chews her lip nervously. I capture her hands in mine. "I won't leave you alone."

Her gaze sweeps across my face. "Okay."

I need Lucca's help, so I'll play nice with him.

I gather up my jacket and tie. "Did Anita show you to a room?"

Mila's eyes narrow slightly before she speaks. "Yeah, she did."

"You don't like her?" I ask, fighting a grin.

"She's okay. She showed me to a room."

"Why don't you show me and we can try to sleep." We leave the pool room.

"Try?"

I like this playful side of Mila. I let my gaze move down her top. "You don't make it easy."

She fires a final smile over her shoulder before she leads the way to our room.

CHAPTER TWENTY FOUR

MILA

Anita left me a high-neck red dress for the party tonight. It cuts off just under my ass. I'm staring at myself in the mirror for far too long, when Nicholai arrives back into the room. His eyes consume me. He looks dangerous in his black slacks and shirt. My stomach flips. His hair is down. I've never seen it like that. As he steps closer, I want to reach up and run my hands through it.

"What is that?" His eyes darken as he reaches me.

"A dress, according to Anita." I try to pull it down, but the material doesn't budge. I've swept all my hair up and only have a light spray of brown across my eyelids.

The red heels Anita left out are too small, but I don't mind padding around barefoot. Nicholai's arm circles my waist, and having no footwear on makes me tiny beside him. I lean out so I can look at him. I do what I have wanted to do the moment he stepped into the room, I run my hands through his dark hair. He bends down and places a soft kiss on my lips that I feel the whole way down to my toes.

"We could skip the party."

I smile into his kiss. "I'm good with that," I answer.

He sighs against my lips. "I'd really love to…" He shrugs and lets me go.

I get it. "We'd better go down."

His gaze dances to my bare feet. "The shoes are too small, and I'm not cramming my feet into them for anyone."

He raises a brow in amusement and recaptures my waist. "Not even for me?" He places another kiss against my lips.

"For you, I would make an exception." I really think if he wanted me to, I would wear them for him.

"You're perfect the way you are."

"Thank God." I grin and his smile has me biting my lip. My mind goes to one place too fast when I'm around Nicholai. No one could blame me. He's magnificent.

The party is being held in a dining room. I didn't realize it would be this kind of party. The table is laid out for a meal. Anita smiles at us. She's wearing a long black dress. I smile back at her. I don't want to. She gave me this cheap dress on purpose. I hold my head high as I walk to the table. Nicholai pulls out my chair, and I smile up at him before sitting down.

I meet Lucca's gaze. His eye color is unusual; I'm not sure if it's silver or gray. Anita is beside Lucca, and two men are already seated at the table, but two more place mats have been set.

"We have two more guests arriving. A friend and his son." Lucca answers my unspoken question.

"Alex and Bogan, this is Mila, Nic's girlfriend." The way Lucca introduces me has amusement in his voice. The two men look at me differently now. If this was real and I was Nicholai's girlfriend, I'd feel ten feet tall, but I have to remember that we're just pretending and not get carried away.

"Lovely to meet you, Mila." I think he's the one called Bogan. He has more tattoos on the left side of his face than his right. You'd expect to see someone like him at a street corner, not at a table in a very expensive house.

"You too." I force a smile and like the feel of Nicholai's hand on my bare thigh.

"How have things been?" Bogan turns his attention to Nicholai, who releases my thigh.

"I've been busy. I see you have moved up the ranks."

Bogan spreads his hands, a grin on his face that displays dimples on either side. "I might be one of The Watchers."

Nicholai's laughter is soft and sends waves through me. "Might be, huh?"

"Are you the other?" Nicholai asks Alex.

"No, I have a different role. But like you and Lucca, I climbed fast too. I knew what I had to do." Alex picks up a glass of clear liquid and sips from it. "What did you do to get your title?"

"The unthinkable," Lucca answers for Nicholai, and my stomach hollows out. What is the unthinkable?

The men laugh around the table, and I have a moment of understanding that I'm seated with the most dangerous members of the Bratva. I should be terrified. I should be trying to escape while they eat and drink, but sitting beside Nicholai, I've never felt so safe in my life.

I glance up at him, and his dark eyes meet mine. I want to know what the unthinkable is.

"Lucca thinks he's funny." Nicholai reaches out, and when his fingers touch my face, I lean into his touch. "But he's not."

Lucca sneers at Nicholai's insult and picks up his drink while saluting Nicholai. For me, I believe Lucca. I think these men did the unthinkable. I've seen Nicholai strangle and shoot a man. I've watched him burn and bury bodies.

The doors open and an elderly man enters with a tray of food. I accept the steak dish, which is the same for everyone. The plates are put down at the two empty spots, and the waiter leaves as the two other men arrive. I'm ready to pick up my knife and fork when everything in me sours. My fingers tighten around the table as blue eyes stare back at me.

"Mila." Eric looks so much older. But it's been six or seven years. He's a man now, but I would know him anywhere. His blond hair and pale skin are still the same, but he's larger, with tattoos snaking up his neck.

I'm standing and moving. His smile melts off his face as I reach him. My hand collides with his cheek, the sound deafening in the room.

His father steps closer. "Mila." The warning is there as his gaze bounces between me and his son.

Eric touches his face, which is already turning red. "I deserved that."

"Nicholai." I freeze as Eric's father says Nicholai's name.

"Vlad." Nicholai's voice is right behind me. His large hands touch my shoulders.

Eric's gaze zones in on the hands on my shoulders. I want to snap my fingers in Eric's face and make him look at me. So much anger I thought I left behind boils and bubbles under my skin.

"You left me for dead." I say the words I know I shouldn't. It isn't the time or place.

Eric's face grows tight. "I searched for you." He takes a step closer toward me, and he's as large as the rest of the men in the room. I feel tiny, but I hold my head high.

"You're such a liar," I spit out, and Nicholai's hands tighten on my shoulder. I glance back at him, and I don't know what warning his eyes hold, but I ignore it and spin back to Eric.

"I hate you."

"My son isn't responsible for your behavior, Miss Ivanov. Your father did what any father would have done."

I grit my teeth at his lies. "You would say that. You always kissed his ass."

I can feel the change in the room and glance at the table as Lucca rises.

"Ivanov?"

My heart starts to pound, and before I can answer, Nicholai blocks me and turns to Lucca. "Who she is doesn't matter. She's here with me, under my protection."

Nicholai's back is rod straight, and I don't see anyone trying to test him. I peek out as Lucca nods.

"Everyone sit."

I don't want to, but I follow Nicholai to the table. I hate that I have to eat beside Eric and his father. They will run to my father the moment they have the chance. Nicholai has got to know that. The tension at the table seems to grow.

"You're Victor's daughter?" Bogan asks, with a smile that shows off his full dimples.

"Yes, I am," I answer, and pick up the glass of clear liquid. It's vodka and I like the taste of it. It reminds me of the man to my left, who's rigid beside me.

"You look good."

I'd throw the glass at Eric if I could get away with it. "Don't speak to me. You lost that privilege when you left me."

"I tried to find you." He speaks again through gritted teeth.

I hate how we have captured the attention of everyone at the table. Anita isn't smiling when I meet her eyes. I'm not sure what I see. Respect? Is it because I'm standing up to Eric or because of who I am?

I snort and drink more vodka. I want to cry, I want to run, but I hold my head high.

"Everyone eat," Lucca's command is said like we aren't all stiff as boards around his table.

The food goes down like dry sand. I empty my glass of vodka and Bogan winks at me as he refills my glass from a jug I thought held water.

This is exactly what happens when people learn who I am. Are they all looking at me as a ticket to a promotion? They did the unthinkable to get where they are today. Did they hand over family members, wives, children? I drink more and want to bark at Eric to stop staring at me.

Silence fills the space as everyone eats. I give up the pretense and just drink. Nicholai eats, and when I glance at him, he looks almost relaxed, like this isn't unusual.

"I swear, Mila, I looked for you."

I push my chair back and pick up my drink before turning to Eric. "Speak to me one more time and you will regret it."

I leave the warning and pad out of the room with my head held high. I had no idea what would transpire after I left, but I didn't think it would be the sound of a gun being fired.

CHAPTER TWENTY FIVE

NICHOLAI

VLAD HITS THE GROUND. I have two guns drawn—one pointed at Vlad's head while he nurses his shoulder, and the other pointed at Eric.

"I'm a perfect shot. That's just a warning." Everyone else is standing, but no one has drawn a gun on me. Vlad was ready to follow Mila from the room, and I couldn't have that. I'm too close to snapping.

"Why don't we lower the guns and talk?" Lucca suggests.

I don't look to Lucca, but he knows how this goes down.

"If they leave this room, they will alert Victor, and I was commissioned to collect Mila. So dropping the gun isn't going to happen, brother."

"What do you need?" His words have relief swimming through me.

"Money and a head start." I have to run. Staying here isn't an option anymore.

"You have it." This time, I look to Lucca and nod.

"You won't get away with this." Vlad still clutches his shoulder, but it's Eric I focus on. He left Mila to rot in the mill. What kind of man does that make him? His face is twisted in rage, and that's what will get him killed one day.

I pull the trigger and he roars, falling to the ground. I've blown out his knee cap. I wanted to blow out his brains, but I'm feeling lenient. Eric doesn't ask why. He has the sense to look away from me.

Lucca taps my shoulder without looking my way. "Bogan, Alex, don't let them move."

Bogan and Alex both stand, extracting guns. I don't relax until I'm outside the room.

"I'll get you some money." Lucca takes the stairs two at a time.

I take out my phone. Mila's dot comes to life beside me. I look around and spot a small door. I open it and find her looking angry and ready to go off on someone. Her face is tearstained as she glances up at me. The vodka pools in her eyes.

"We have to go." I reach in and pull her off the toilet seat. Her glass is empty.

"I want another drink." She wipes her tears away with the back of her hand. I hate the effect Eric has on her. I hate the hurt that twists her beautiful face. I'm tempted to go back into the room and end him.

Lucca races down the stairs with a duffle bag that I catch. Digging into his pocket, he clutches a set of keys before throwing them at me.

"She's parked out front."

I tighten my fingers around the keys. "I can't thank you enough."

Lucca pulls me into a hug. "You saved me more times in prison."

"We saved each other," I say.

Lucca nods. "They'll send me after you," he states. "I'll come."

I grin at him. "I wouldn't expect anything less from you, brother."

Lucca turns to Mila. "You take care of him. He's one of the good guys."

I laugh, but Mila doesn't answer. I think she's gone beyond playing nice.

"I hope she's worth it," Lucca says.

"She is," I answer before leaving Lucca's house behind. I unlock the slick black car, and Mila gets into the passenger seat. She's still clutching the empty glass. She places it between her legs as she buckles herself in.

"I'm sorry." She speaks when we're on the road.

I glance at her. "For what?"

"I should have stayed silent." Her eyes meet mine.

"I would never expect you to remain silent, Mila. I can see he hurt you."

She quickly looks away from me and falls silent again for a few more moments.

"I heard gunshots."

I flicker my gaze to Mila. She's watching me intently.

"Vlad was about to follow you."

Her deep inhale of breath has me regretting telling her. I have to remember this isn't the life she was born into. She was born into the more blanketed part of Bratva.

"Is he dead?" She doesn't sound upset.

"Nah, it was only a flesh wound."

"I heard two gunshots." Her voice is low, and her eyes are drowning in sorrow.

"The second was for Eric."

I can see the pulse in her neck flicker to life.

Before she asks me if he's dead, I tell her, "Another wound. Not lethal, but serious enough to cause pain."

I focus on the road and let Mila delve deep into her thoughts. I have no idea where we're going—I'm running. The Collector doesn't run. Ever. But I just need some time to figure out what to do.

"Did you shoot him for me?" she asks nervously.

I smile instantly. "Yes."

I glance at her, and she nods at me. "Thank you."

I grin. "You are welcome."

She has no idea what I would do for her—what I have done for her already and would do in the future to keep her safe. I wasn't exactly overly confident about how safe I could keep her when it came to Victor. You don't stand up to the leader of the Bratva and live.

Lucca asking me if she was worth it means he knws the price I will pay for this.

I glance at Mila again. She's rolling the empty vodka glass in her hands. Her legs are drawn up on the seat. She's beautiful.

Yes. She's worth it.

CHAPTER TWENTY SIX

MILA

S EEING ERIC DID SOMETHING to me. Even as I heard the string of gunshots, I didn't run like I should have. I sat in that bathroom and cried angry tears while wondering if he was bleeding out on the floor. I take a peek at Nicholai. He's focused on the road, and I have no idea what we're doing. Him shooting Eric wouldn't be brushed off. Shooting Vlad is a crime I can't see my father forgiving. I got Nicholai into this mess.

"If I wanted to see my father, I had to schedule an appointment with his security." My words don't matter now. We have bigger problems, but I can't stop the anger that's spinning through my mind.

"I made an appointment the morning of my seventeenth birthday to have breakfast with him." I roll the glass in my hand.

"I mean, it was scheduled, but he canceled at the last minute." I remember trying to eat the pancakes alone without crying. That night, I went off with Eric and we snuck into a VIP venue and ate all the free food. We could have gotten in, but it was far more fun breaking the rules.

"I'm sorry, Mila."

I glance at Nicholai and shrug. "It doesn't matter now."

"What happened the day you got sent to the mill?"

"I told you, I stole a car with Eric."

The car slows down, and Nicholai pulls off to the side of the road. "I know this isn't easy, but tell me what happened."

I want to ask him why this is important to him.

I glance down and roll the glass in between my hands again.

"I was called to my father's office. The man we stole the car from was a friend of my father's, so he wasn't going to report it. My father was pretty pissed."

I knew things were bad when I was summoned to his office. He'd never asked me to come before. A small part of me thought, just maybe, he wanted to make up for all the missed birthdays, all the dinners I ate with our staff, or maybe he just realized there was more to this life than work. No, he wanted to punish me.

"He had been informed by my bodyguard of all the things Eric and I had gotten into. I hadn't known Dimitri was reporting everything..."

"Dimitri?" Nicholai is frowning.

"Yeah. So that was the final straw for my father. His daughter embarrassing him."

I glance out the window as trickles of rain hit the glass. "Eric never got punished. Just me."

I turn back to Nicholai, who gives me an encouraging look to continue. "He said I was going to the mill as punishment and that he would send The Collector when he felt my lesson was learned. I had heard of the mill, so at first I didn't believe him. I even went willingly with Oleg."

"Oleg took you there?" Nicholai asks.

"Yeah. When we arrived at the mill, the reality sank in. I was placed in a small room with Liddi, and I waited each day for you to come." My damp fingers leave an imprint on the glass. "A week later, Oleg arrived and we got into an argument, so he left without me. He kept coming back to sleep with Liddi, though, and he never took me with him."

Liddi's screams invade my mind again, and I push them away. "A week later, after he killed Liddi, he returned. He told me my father wanted me to disappear, so he gave me money and dropped me off. That was it."

"You never tried to contact your father?" Nicholai is frowning.

"Why would I? He didn't want me. He never had. It was a second chance at a better life."

Nicholai starts the car and does a full U-turn. "Why are we going back?" I ask him.

"I need to check something."

I focus on his tattooed hands, which are clenched on the steering wheel. I want to tell him he should walk away from this, from me, but I don't. I'm selfish as I stare out the window and hope he doesn't abandon me like everyone else in my life has.

The alcohol lulls me into a half sleep. I'm aware of the car moving under us. I'm aware when it slows down and comes to a stop. I sit up straight as I look around the neighborhood.

"Where are we?"

"I need you to stay in the car." Nicholai stares up at the house that's three stories tall. It's a fancy townhouse. I know wealth when I see it.

Nicholai gets out and closes the door. The moment he does, I lock the car from the inside, not wanting to be hijacked again. The time ticks by, and I start to grow nervous as I glare up at the house. I don't see any movement. I flip down the visor and wipe away the small amount of mascara from under my eyes. My eyes are red from crying and alcohol. I do what I can before closing the visor and waiting.

The car heats up, and I hate feeling trapped. Opening the door, I let some air in but am ready to close it if anyone comes. I see movement at the top window. My heart races, and I close the door gently like whoever is up there might hear me. I'm staring at the same window but nothing moves. Maybe it was a trick of the light?

My heart lifts as Nicholai approaches the car. I unlock it and he climbs in. Without a word, he starts to drive away from the house.

"You want to explain to me what that was all about?"

He reaches into his jacket pocket and pulls out a folded-up photo. "Is that Dimitri, your bodyguard?"

I take the photo. Dimitri is in it with the woman we met on the street, Gail, and a young girl about six, who is smiling up at the camera.

"Yeah, that's him." I look up to Nicholai. "Small world," I say.

Nicholai takes the picture back. He removes something else from his pocket and hands it to me. "Can you read that?"

I take the white slip of paper and open it. I glance at Nicholai for an explanation.

"Just read it." He's focused on the road.

My stomach squirms.

"Primary School, St. Mary's Convent, Crews Hill Street. I give Irina Smirnov permission to go on the school field trip the 23rd of August."

I take another glance at Nicholai. "Signed Dimitri and Gail Smirnov. He was married and had a child?" I frown at the permission slip.

Nicholai doesn't speak but keeps driving. I want an explanation. What does it matter that he was married to Gail? Only, Gail had sent men to kill Nicholai. Why? None of it made sense.

"To leave the Bratva, you can't just walk away," Nicholai says. "He must have done something..."

"Unthinkable," I say what Lucca had said.

Nicholai glances at me before focusing on the road. "We can't outrun this, so I need you to trust me."

I'm nodding. "I do." I haven't known him long, but I trust Nicholai completely. He kept me safe, when the people I grew up with hadn't.

"I'm going to ask you to do something for me, and I know you won't like it."

I swallow but nod. "I'll do it."

Nicholai's gaze roams across my body. "We need to get you some clothes."

I try to pull the material down my thigh, but it's no use. The dress is tiny and doesn't cover much, so I'm happy to get out of it.

Once again, I wait in the car as Nicholai enters a large store to get me some clothes. I'm nervous. I have no idea what he will ask of me. I won't kill anyone or do anything sexual. That's where I draw the line. Guilt swirls in my stomach at thinking such things about Nicholai. I don't believe he would ask me to do either.

Nicholai comes back out fifteen minutes later with one bag. He glances at his watch before handing me the bag. "Can you get dressed as I drive?"

I'm already pulling out the denim jeans. The car starts and we're driving.

I put on the socks and boots before removing the red dress. I glance at Nicholai to find him watching me. After pulling on the cream jumper, I let my hair down. His nod of approval shouldn't send my stomach into knots.

"Gail and Dimitri's daughter will finish school in five minutes. I want you to approach her and bring her back to the car."

I'm already shaking my head. "You want me to kidnap a child?" Is he crazy?

"We need her." Nicholai doesn't flinch, and I see no remorse in his dark eyes.

"No," I say.

"If I get out and approach a little girl, it will look suspicious."

"I don't care. I'm not doing it."

Nicholai drives faster and pulls up outside a set of black iron gates. A few meters in is the forbidding convent that's a primary school.

"Listen to me. We need that little girl. That's the only way Gail will tell me what's going on."

"You need to figure out another way." I hate the look in his eyes, but kidnapping a child? I just can't do it.

"It's not kidnapping. She will be with her mother straight away. We take her from here to her mother. It's just so Gail answers my questions."

Nicholai takes my hands in his. "I can't see any other way out. I believe Gail is involved in all this. I think what's happening to you has nothing to do with your father."

I frown and try to remove my hands from Nicholai's, but he doesn't let them go. "Do you want to die, Mila?"

"Of course not."

"Then get that girl or we are both dead." My heart pounds and I glance up at the school. The main doors open and small little people pour out. Nicholai releases my hands.

"Take another look." I stare at the photo and my stomach sickens.

"She will be with her mother in fifteen minutes. No harm will come to her."

I look into Nicholai's eyes. He wouldn't lie to me. I have to trust him.

I nod. "Okay, I'll do it."

CHAPTER TWENTY SEVEN

NICHOLAI

S HE APPEARS SHIFTY AS she glances over all the students before throwing a frightened look over her shoulder toward me. She has no idea how terrified she looks. If she doesn't tone it down, she will draw unwanted attention to herself. Her hands knot together behind her back, and she takes a step toward the children. They run in all directions and part around her stiff frame as she takes another step toward our target.

Irina tilts her head and stares up at Mila. Mila must be smiling; I can't tell as she has her back to me, but Irina is smiling back. I glance around the space, but no one is paying attention to Irina or Mila. I still want her to hurry up. She's taking far too long. Mila is bent over slightly. Now she's standing and reaching out her hand. Irina takes it and they start to walk toward the car. Mila's gaze meets mine, and I hold her stare. If I let it go, I fear she will release the child. I hold her gaze firmly as she opens the back door of the car and Irina jumps in.

She assesses me as she clips in her seat belt.

"I liked my old driver." Her voice rings older than a six-year-old.

"You'll get used to me," I tell her and start the car. Mila gets into the passenger seat, and as she's putting on her seat belt, I pull away from the curb.

"How was school?" Mila's voice shakes slightly, and I want to tell her not to speak to the child, that it makes this more difficult.

"Some classes are interesting, others not so much."

I glance at Irina in the rearview mirror. She really doesn't speak like a six-year-old.

"Mila said you're taking me home. I have horse riding lessons first, so you can take me to the farm."

She's rummaging through her backpack. When she takes a silver device out of her bag, I swing around and take it from her hand.

"Excuse me?"

I ignore her outrage and flip open the phone. "Who are you going to ring?"

She rolls her eyes. "My horse trainer, to tell her I'm going to be a bit late."

"You don't have horse riding lessons, sweetie," Mila says and she turns in her seat so she can see Irina. "We are taking you straight to your mam."

I lied when I told her I would take Irina back to Gail. That isn't going to happen until I get what I want.

"Actually, we're taking a detour."

"We are?" Mila speaks through gritted teeth.

"Gail wants a word with me alone."

Mila scoffs and glares out the window. I peek down at her tightened fists. Guilt rolls in my stomach at lying to her, but I had no choice.

I drive down the side of the hotel and park. "What are we doing?" Mila sounds alarmed.

I need her to stay calm. "It's just for a few hours."

"You said…" Mila doesn't finish her sentence as she glances back at Irina, who removes her seat belt and picks up her backpack.

"A few hours. That's all I ask." I try to keep my voice low.

Mila shakes her head with disgust in her eyes. I grip her hand. "I need you to tell me you're with me on this."

She pulls her hand from mine. "I have no other choice." She gets out, and I accept her answer. We walk along the side of the building, and Mila takes Irina's hand.

"Shouldn't we be using the front door?" Irina asks.

"They're doing some construction close to the front door," Mila says, "so we have to use the back door instead, sweetie."

We reach a side door, and I knock three times. It opens. The chef takes one look at me and steps back, giving us entry. Everyone knows who I am—sometimes that comes with perks, like now.

We move through the noisy kitchen.

"Everyone comes through the kitchen?" Irina's voice is filled with disbelief. The child is far too clever.

"No, just us," Mila answers her. "We're special."

I stop at the back door that leads to the stairs up to the rooms.

"You go on up and wait for me. I'll just book us in."

Mila won't meet my eyes, but she smiles at Irina and leads her up the stairs. I step out of the service hall and into the hustle of the main area of the hotel.

I can't disguise myself—that's the downside of being who I am. I don't intend to stay here for long. I get a room and slip back through the service door, up the back stairs that are only used for the cleaning staff.

Mila and Irina are sitting on a long red velvet couch in one of the wide hallways. Mila meets my eyes, and she shakes her head but stands.

I search for our room number and find it is only three doors down. I enter the small space. It's clean and has some bottles of water sitting on the round table under the window. I immediately check to see if anyone looks suspicious outside.

"Irina, why don't you start your homework. I want to have a chat with Nicholai."

Turning back, Mila is waiting for me. Irina is sitting at the table removing books from her bag. I follow Mila outside the hotel room door.

"How could you?" she starts the moment we're out of the hotel room.

"I had no choice…" I start to say.

"You lied to me. You had a choice. You could have told me the truth!" Her words grow loud, and I step in closer to make her lower her voice.

"If I had told you the truth, you wouldn't have agreed."

She folds her arms across her chest, and her blue eyes swim with pain. I want to reach out and kiss her. I want to comfort her and take away some of the hurt I've caused. "No, I wouldn't have agreed. This is wrong."

"It's done. I need you to stay with her while I speak to Gail."

Mila looks at me with disbelief. "I'm taking part in a kidnapping." She nods her head in disbelieve. "What happens when things go wrong with Gail?"

"Mila, nothing is going to happen to the child."

She unfolds her arms. "You also told me we would take her to her mam. So, I'm struggling to believe you."

Her words are ground out, and I'm tempted to kiss her and end this, but I don't think my kiss would be a warm welcome right now.

"We are wasting time. They have to know she's missing. They will have already started to search for her."

Mila's face pales. "Are we in danger?"

"If I don't leave now and confront Gail, I might lose too much time. So can you do as I asked? Can you stay with her?"

Mila nods her head and looks away from me. I want to reach out and force her to look at me, but she steps back into the room. Irina's head snaps up, and she narrows her eyes at me before returning to her homework.

"I won't be long." Mila steps away from me as I try to reach her.

I'm wasting time, but I hate seeing her closed off from me.

"Mila," I say softly, and she finally looks at me.

"I won't be long." I settle on the words that weren't the ones I intended to use. I wanted to tell her I'm doing this for us—for her. That I'm doing this because I love her.

CHAPTER TWENTY EIGHT

MILA

I CHECK THE FRIDGE, which holds a pack of peanuts and a chocolate bar. I take out the bar and give it to Irina. She opens the candy without a word as I pour her a glass of water. I can't stop listening for pounding footsteps. I'm imagining a group of thugs with guns drawn searching the halls for us. Sweat coats my palms, and I rub them on my pants. The sound of Irina munching on the candy calms my heart a bit. I sit on the bed. This is wrong. We shouldn't have taken a child.

"Will you be picking me up from school from now on?" Irina continues to write in her notepad as she asks me the question that makes me feel sick with guilt.

"No, sweetie. It's just for today." Saliva pools in my mouth at my words. I've taken part in kidnapping a child. I get off the bed. She will be with her mam in a few hours and this will be over. She will remember doing her homework while eating a candy bar. That's what I tell myself, anyway.

"Can I watch TV?" she asks.

I smile at Irina. "Of course."

She quickly slides out of her chair and sits on the bed. I sit beside her with the remote and flick through the stations until I come across a cartoon.

"I don't watch them." She frowns up at me.

I keep going until she tells me to stop at some nature program.

I get up and let her watch her program and walk to the window to see if Nicholai has returned. I know it's stupid; he only recently left. Glancing out the window, my heart pounds as a sleek black car pulls up across from the hotel. It's not Nicholai.

I'm ready to dismiss the car when all four doors open and men get out. There's nothing identifying about them. They all wear black, but I've been around the wrong kind of men long enough to know what I'm looking at. I let the curtain go and step back from the window. My attention draws to Irina. What if they're here for her? Would they kill me? I could be overreacting, but my gut is telling me I need to run.

"Take off your jumper." Irina reluctantly looks away from the TV and to me. She doesn't do as I ask and I'm moving.

"Take off your jumper."

She does this time, and I quickly remove the navy school tie. The blue shirt doesn't look as stark as the navy jumper with her school's logo embroidered on the front.

"We need to leave." She doesn't question me, and when I stop her from getting her school bag, she follows me out the door. I take her hand and calmly walk back toward the service door that should lead us back into the kitchen. My heart pounces in my chest as a couple walks toward us. They look normal, but they could be undercover. I tighten my hold on Irina and am tempted to reach up and wipe the sweat that's gathering on the back of my neck. The woman smiles at Irina, and I tug her closer to my leg as we move past them.

"Why are we leaving?" Irina's question has my heart racing further.

"We just need to," I say as I push open the large wooden door that leads to the stairs. The sound of heavy footfalls has me pulling Irina behind me. I glance over the rails and catch a glimpse of four men dressed in black. Panic claws at me, and I'm dragging Irina back into the hallway, half running. I keep looking over my shoulder.

We catch up with the couple at the elevators, and the woman gives me a look of suspicion. I try to calm down and force a wobbly smile. I press the button again for the elevator. What is taking so long?

My stomach lifts as the ding of the doors has us stepping through. I look up to see the four men step into the hallway. The first one has a scar running along his cheek. He reaches behind his back, and my instincts have me pulling Irina behind me to protect her. As the doors close, I see what he removed.

A phone.

The music in the elevator is painfully calming and instrumental. I glance at the woman who hasn't taken her eyes off me.

"You in trouble, sweetheart?"

I'm ready to deny it but look at the man who is with her. They're both in their fifties, both seem respectable.

"The man with the scar? You seemed afraid of him?"

"Wendy, this is none of our business."

Wendy ignores the man, who I assume is her husband.

All it will take is for Irina to spill the truth, but I take my chances. "Yeah, he's an ex."

Sweat makes a pathway down my back as the elevator comes to a halt. The doors open and we step out into the lobby. I freeze as two men dressed in black block the main door.

"Are those men with your ex?" Wendy is beside me and I nod.

"Go get security," Wendy tells her husband, and I'm ready to scramble after him to stop him, but he's already making his way to the desk.

"I won't leave you." Wendy holds firm, and it's a reminder that there are still good people in the world.

But I don't believe for one second that will help us. I turn back around and drag Irina with me. Pushing open a door, we enter another long hallway. I can hear Wendy call after us. But she can't help.

I start to jog, and Irina jogs with me. I glance down at the little girl that has come willingly through all of this.

She stops running, and I've been waiting for her to rebel and ask me what's happening. I'm ready to give this six-year-old the best explanation I can when she speaks first.

"We can pull the fire alarm, cause a distraction, and get out."

I'm at a loss for words. Reaching up, I take the small steel weapon that hangs along the side of the fire alarm. I smash the glass, then push the button, and red lights swirl to life along with a roaring sound. Doors open and people fill the hallways. I turn back around and follow the crowd back out into the lobby.

I want to ask Irina how she knew to do that, but right now my focus is getting out of this place.

Wendy meets my eyes in the lobby, and I'm surprised when she falls into step beside us, shielding us from onlookers. We shuffle through the main door and out into the fresh air. The wail of fire engines and cop cars grow louder, and the street in front of the hotel turns into a circus we can disappear in.

"Thank you," I say to Wendy before pushing deeper into the crowd with Irina. We get swallowed up and spit out along the sidewalk as we fall into step with shoppers. I can only hope we blend in well enough until Nicholai finds us.

CHAPTER TWENTY NINE

NICHOLAI

I GAIN ENTRY TO Gail's house like she already knows I'm coming. That makes me nervous. Withdrawing my gun, I enter her kitchen. She's standing at the end of the counter holding a full glass of wine that hasn't been touched. She's trying to appear calm, and that tells me she must be aware of her daughter's disappearance. I'm tempted to take out my phone and check for Mila again, but I had before coming in here and she was at the hotel.

"Nicholai, you took my daughter." This time Gail drinks from her glass.

"No harm will come to her." I slowly lower my gun. She has no weapons that I can see, and I don't think she'll kill me, not knowing where her daughter is.

"I have men searching for her right now, Nicholai." Gail places the glass back onto the counter. Her eyes are on fire with anger that she's fighting not to display.

"I need answers. You told me I pissed off some pretty powerful people. I want to know who." I close the back door behind me before stepping into the kitchen.

"If any harm comes to my daughter..."

"That's up to you, Gail," I snap back, knowing she's wasting time. Time isn't a luxury I have right now. "Now, answer my questions and I will let your daughter go."

"How many times do you think my daughter has been kidnapped?" The question is delivered with a raised brow. Gail drinks deeply from her glass.

"Three times," she answers her own question. "Those three times, the men who took her died a slow and painful death."

"You can keep threatening me, but they won't find your daughter. I'm not stupid, Gail." I itch to check my phone again. What if they found Mila? She would be dead. I don't think they would have found her that fast.

I have to believe I still have time.

"Who ordered the kill on me, Gail?" I withdraw my gun again, wanting her to answer quickly.

"Oleg." That confirms my suspicions.

"Why?"

"When you have all your answers, then what?"

I cock the gun. "Then I leave here and you get your daughter back."

Gail holds my eye, and I have no idea what's going on inside her head. She's a clever woman.

"I don't know why he ordered your death. I was happy to assist since you killed Dimitri. You were just meant to deliver him to the can, and from there, I knew I would get him back. But you killed him instead."

"What do you mean, get him back?" No one came back from the can.

Gail steps closer to me, completely ignoring the gun I still have pointed in her direction.

She exhales loudly. "Dimitri got out of the Bratva by doing a favor for Oleg. I didn't learn about that favor until a few years ago. Dimitri helped cover up the disappearance of Victor's daughter."

She's talking about Mila.

"But I think someone discovered the girl, and Dimitri was being brought in for questioning. Oleg said it was standard and that he collected everyone from the can, so he would make sure Dimitri was safe." Gail's hands curl around the counter. "Only he wasn't."

The fire returns to her eyes, and I don't want her thinking about Dimitri; I want her to stay focused.

"What do you think Victor would do if he was aware you held this knowledge?"

Gail's face pales. "I just want my daughter back. I had no hand in his daughter. None."

Her voice rises and I hold up a hand, feeling accomplished in what I wanted to do—take her mind off Dimitri.

"It's not looking good for you, Gail, conspiring with Oleg."

"You killed Dimitri, and I was happy to assist with your death. I still am."

I grin at her honesty.

It makes sense how Dimitri got away from Bratva. I wondered who had alerted Oleg to Mila's whereabouts. Now I'm questioning who sent me the order to collect her. Was Oleg hoping she would try to escape and I'd kill her and then he would wipe me out?

"You sent your men to my home to kill me. Was that the only order?"

Gail looks away for the first time. "No. Oleg gave me specific instructions to send them into a front living space, where a girl was being held. She was to be killed too."

"Do you know who she is?" I raise the gun at Gail.

"No, but I think I can figure it out."

The phone starts to ring, and Gail looks to it. I point at the phone with my gun. "Answer it, and put it on speaker."

Gail doesn't look away from me as she opens the phone and places it on speaker.

"Did you get her?" Gail asks.

Sirens wail in the background. "They got away. She's with a blonde woman. They pulled the fire alarm in the hotel, and I think others are working with them."

I take my own phone out of my pocket and open it up. Mila's dot is moving. She's a few blocks away from the hotel.

"Did you see Irina?" Gail's voice betrays her emotion for the first time.

"Yes, boss. She's fine. We'll get her."

"You better," Gail snarls before ending the call.

"I'll have her back to you within the hour," I say. "You can call off your men. Mila witnessed a murder of a young girl by Oleg. That's why he's trying to make her disappear without dirtying his hands."

"Why are you telling me this?" Gail clutches the phone in her hand.

"Helping him isn't about Dimitri. He would have killed Dimitri anyway. He knew too much. Maybe I gave him mercy."

"You burned his body. I couldn't even have a final goodbye!" Her angry words fuel her steps. "He won't stop!" Gail fires out.

"I know." I know Oleg won't stop coming for me or Mila. "Call off your men," I say, as my own fear for Mila grows.

"No."

"I will deliver your daughter back here."

"You think I will heel just like that?"

"Yes, if you know what is good for you." I raise the gun.

I see it in Gail's eyes. She won't submit. "If you were going to shoot me, Nic, you would have already done it."

She's right. I don't want to leave a child orphaned.

I put the gun away and slip back out through the back door. Talking to Gail didn't solve my problem. Mila and I were targets, and that didn't change. But at least I know who's behind it and why. I'm not stupid to think that Gail won't have me followed. I take out my phone as I drive and check to see where Mila is. She's at a park.

I keep checking the rearview mirror to make sure I'm not being followed. I'm not surprised when a black jeep takes a left, right, and another left just as I do. I wait until I'm coming up to a red light before I stomp on the gas pedal. Horns blow as he tries to follow me but gets stuck behind the red light.

I take off and continue zigzagging through the city until I'm sure I'm not being followed. I dump the car close to the park and start to walk.

CHAPTER THIRTY

MILA

IRINA WALKS BESIDE ME like we do this all the time. As we pass the swings, she stops. "I never get to go to the park. I never get to go on the swings."

"Why don't you have a go now?" I smile at her encouragingly. Us delaying isn't wise, but my heart squeezes. What child hasn't been to the park?

"No, I'm fine," she answers me while staring at the swings. I step away from her and sit on one of the swings.

"What are you doing?" She's trying to look serious, but I can see the child in her eyes. The one that wants to join me.

"I like swinging." I push myself higher and don't look at Irina. She soon gives up her protest and joins me on the swings. Her laughter is musical, and guilt churns in the pit of my stomach at what I'm taking part in.

I slow down and just watch her as she becomes the six-year-old she clearly never gets to be. I cast my gaze around the empty park. My stomach twists, and something deep inside me stirs as Nicholai walks toward us. Irina slows down on the swing.

I'm still seated on the swing when Nicholai approaches. I'm waiting for him to stop his approach, but he doesn't. He reaches me and bends my head back. His gaze roams my face before he presses his lips against mine. It's harsh and quick, but I feel it all the way to my toes.

"We have to go," he says the moment he breaks the kiss.

"Irina goes home now?" I don't move off the swing, and Nicholai shakes his head.

"Not right now."

I'm standing and shaking my head. "No, Nicholai. She's a kid." I step away from the swings.

Irina is moving slowly, listening to us, and her mind might be sharpened to adult conversations, but I would treat her like a six-year-old.

"This was wrong from the start," I say.

"Gail gave me some answers, but we could use her to get more."

I reach up and touch Nicholai's face. "If you think anything of me, you will let Irina go. Please! I'm begging you."

I see the turmoil in Nicholai's dark eyes, and when he looks away from me, I drag his face back to mine. "Please."

I'm begging with everything in me.

Nicholai steps out of my touch, and my heart starts to crumble. He takes out his phone and dials a number. His gaze swings around the park.

"She's at Park High, sitting on the swing." He ends the call and reaches for me.

"Now we go."

"We can't just leave her, Nicholai."

"I've told Gail where she is. When they get here, we won't walk away from this."

My heart bounces around my chest as I look back to Irina. I walk back to her, and she stops swinging.

"You're going now?"

I nod my head. "Yes, your mam is on her way. So stay on the swing, okay?"

Irina nods. "Thanks for bringing me to the park." Her smile twists at me.

"Take care, and don't leave the swings."

I want to hug her, but Nicholai calls me. It's time to go. I leave Irina on the swing and take off with Nicholai.

"We need to get off the streets." Nicholai curls his hand around mine, but my mind is still back with Irina. Did anyone collect her? Would she be left sitting there alone?

"We shouldn't have left her," I say softly.

"Gail will have her already."

Nicholai's hand tightens on mine. "You did well escaping the hotel. I didn't think they would find you so quickly."

I glance up at Nicholai to see pride shining in his eyes. "It was Irina's idea to pull the fire alarm," I tell him.

His grin is instant. "She sure is Gail's daughter."

"What did you find out?" I ask. I need to take my mind off the little girl on the swing. I have to believe she's safely with her mother now.

We leave the main street and slip down an alleyway. Nicholai knocks on a large steel door and it grinds open. Without a word, he walks through, bringing me with him. A guy with a bald head and tank top grunts at me before pulling the door behind us. We step into a bar that's dimly lit. Nicholai walks to the back booth. He lets me in first before sliding in across from me.

"We'll be safe here, for now."

"Nic, great to see you." A man steps up to the table. He's so thin—to the stage of resembling a walking corpse. His caved-in cheeks are gaunt, and he appears ready to keel over.

"You too, Carson." Nic takes Carson's outstretched hand.

"Manny is on the door. Any trouble, and we will alert you."

Nic nods. "Thanks, Carson."

"I'll get you the usual?"

Nicholai jerks his chin out to me. "Make that two."

Carson smiles. His face is too small for all the teeth he flashes me before leaving.

"He's loyal," Nicholai states and shrugs out of his suit jacket. I take in his tanned forearms as he rolls up his sleeves. My stomach squirms when his eyes meet mine.

"I know today wasn't easy, but it was necessary."

I don't agree, but I don't argue. "What did you learn?"

Nicholai nods like he knows I'm still not happy. "Dimitri helped cover up your disappearance, which tells me that your father doesn't know where you are. They must have made up a story and Dimitri backed up Oleg."

Betrayal courses through me. I wasn't exactly close to Dimitri, but he had been my bodyguard my whole life. "But why?" I wasn't a threat. I was a child then. Why would they want to get rid of me?

"Dimitri wanted out of the Bratva, so he lied to gain his freedom. Why did Oleg do it?" Nicholai shrugs. "I don't know. Do you remember ever having any other interactions with him?"

I'm already shaking my head. "I barely saw my father, never mind Oleg. I took no part in any of it."

"Someone from your past spotted you, which is why Oleg wanted you collected."

Once again I can't think of anyone who cared. My mind immediately jumps to Eric, but I dismiss that fantasy that I had held onto for far too long.

Carson arrives back with a tray carrying two piping hot beef pies. The scent from the pies wafts toward us and its mouthwatering. He places a pie in front of each of us, along with cutlery. He leaves and returns with drinks.

Nicholai starts to eat like we aren't running for our lives. Maybe having this one moment as something normal would be nice? I unroll the knife and fork from the napkin and start to eat. My stomach appreciates the pie.

"Wow," I say after a few forkfuls.

I glance up at Nicholai. He's smiling at me, and my heart jumps around in my chest. We eat in silence, and no matter how hard I try, I can't stop thinking about Irina.

"How does Gail come into all this?" I ask.

"I collected Dimitri and he ran."

The pie in my stomach sours. "And you caught him?" My words are slow, and the moment I say them, I know how stupid they are.

"Yes, I did. So, she was angry and happily teamed up with Oleg to kill me and you."

"Oleg wanted me dead?" Oleg wanted both of us dead, I remind myself. "Nicholai," I start and he holds his hands up like he knows what I might say.

"Let's eat our pie."

We do it in silence, and I take the time to study Nicholai in this lighting. If I saw him in a bar, I would admire him but walk the other way. Trouble is written all over him. Not trouble, but danger. That's what I see when I look at him—a very dangerous man.

Carson arrives at the table. "They're searching for you a few doors down."

Nicholai pulls his jacket back on and thanks Carson. Our quiet moment is gone as we leave through a back door, where four men wait for us. I glance back at Carson and feel the betrayal toward Nicholai, who seemed to have trusted him. Carson shrugs and pulls the steel door behind him. The four men move in closer. The one with the scar on his face glares at me.

This isn't good.

Nicholai pushes me behind him before stepping toward the men.

"I'm going to give you a chance to leave and return to your families." Nicholai's hands hang at his side. I know how good he is, but four men against him, and they all have guns? I have faith in Nicholai, but I'm not naïve either.

"The girl is back with Gail," I say from behind Nicholai.

The guy with the scar sneers at me. "After I kill him, I'm going to gut you slowly."

I move back until my back hits the steel door. I glance around the alleyway for a weapon but turn up empty. Boxes and trash cans are the only things around us. Nicholai bends his head as if he might start to pray. His arms are wide and he looks up.

"Fine." One word falls from his lips before he kicks into action.

It happens so fast. Two of the men with guns drawn hit the ground. A knife pokes out of each one's head. Nicholai reaches up and withdraws two guns from the band of his trousers. He fires quickly.

The other men were stunned momentarily, so he hits one and the other dives before twisting midair and firing back. I hit the ground hard and cover my head. Keeping my eyes tightly closed, I try to disappear into the asphalt. When the sound of gunfire ceases, I finally open my eyes. Nicholai stands and places the guns back into his trousers. Bodies litter the alleyway. I'm being picked up off the ground as Nicholai pats down my body.

"Are you hurt?"

I shake my head as my gaze skitters across all the bodies. Taking my hand, Nicholai takes angry steps along the alleyway and up to the front of the building. He releases me as he runs toward the door, then kicks it in. People slow down to see what all the commotion is about as Nicholai enters the building.

"Don't run, Carson," he calls, and I'm rushing behind him.

"We need to go," I say to Nicholai, not wanting to see any more bloodshed.

Nicholai keeps walking. "You son of a bitch." He marches to the back of the building. Sirens wail in the distance.

"Nicholai, we need to go."

He curses and looks up at me.

"Now!"

He takes one final look at the surrounding space before we leave through the front door.

CHAPTER THIRTY ONE

NICHOLAI

Carson the traitor. I don't want to leave the pub. I want to return and kill him. Mila's small hand rests in mine, and I relax at her touch.

"Going back isn't an option."

Her words make me smile. It's like she's been running her whole life. Most women would have run screaming, but Mila is here holding my hand. I glance down at her just as my phone beeps. I take it out of my pocket and open the message. It's an order to deliver Mila to the can.

"Who is it?"

I'm not sure why she asks. Maybe she can see the tension in my tight jaw? I relax my mouth.

"I have to deliver you to the can," I say honestly.

Mila stops walking. "And if you don't?"

She blinks rapidly, like she's trying to make this situation disappear. I want to reach out and touch her, but I can't while we're standing here on the street.

"Come on." I start to walk again, and I don't have an answer for her. If I don't deliver her, someone will be sent after us. There is no stopping the wheels that are turning. Right now, I need to get Mila somewhere safe.

The motel is run down, and the stench has me reconsidering staying here with Mila, but our choices are limited. It won't be for long. I know what I need to do to keep her safe.

"You don't have to do this." Her voice sounds bruised, and I give her a tired smile.

"I know." I close the door of the motel room and circle my arms around her. "I want to do this." I place a kiss on her forehead and pull her into me. I love her, and letting her go isn't an option.

"They will kill us"—she's shaking her head against my chest—"if you don't deliver me to the can." She leans out and pain swirls in her eyes. "We can't keep running."

"I know." I release her and weigh my words. Do I tell her the truth about what I'm going to do? I glance at Mila and decide she deserves the truth.

"I'm going to the can," I say.

She folds her arms across her small chest as she tries to hide the pain I see flicker in her eyes. She must think I'm going to deliver her to the can.

"I'm going to deliver myself to the can," I clarify. The horror of my confession on her face has me smiling.

"I need to be taken to Victor. It's the only way to end this."

She's shaking her head. "No, you can't go. My father... you have no idea what kind of man he is." Her voice rises in disgust.

I take her in my arms again. "I know what kind of man he is, Mila. I work for him. I know the unthinkable things I do for him. This is the only way."

She's shaking her head again like we have a choice. Time is against us, and I decide to use these few moments the way I really want to. Pressing my lips against Mila's gives me the desired effect I want. She melts into me, and I hope for the next while I can make her forget.

My tongue slips easily between her lips, and her warmth surrounds me. She moans into my mouth, and my cock grows harder. The smell of the motel room penetrates my lust, and I break the kiss. She's panting, and I love how her eyes are swimming with a want I can fill.

I take her hand, and she doesn't question as I lead her outside. It's still bright, yet the light from the day is starting to dim. We don't have the full disguise of the dark, but that makes it more exciting as I lead us down the alleyway. I go deeply enough that we can't be seen from the parking lot. When I stop, Mila frowns.

"What are you doing?"

I answer with a kiss that presses her back into the brick wall. She hesitates, and when I press my hard cock against her, she wraps her arms around my neck and pulls me closer. I slip my hand down her trousers, and she groans into my mouth as I dip my finger into her soaking pussy. I want to taste her sweetness. Taking up my hand,

I give myself what I want and suck each finger. Her pussy tastes sweeter than I remember.

"I want you inside me." Her frantic words are delivered with her dragging my hand back to her. I rub the outside of her dampening trousers.

"Aren't you worried someone will see us?" I question before nipping her earlobe.

"I don't care."

That's exactly what I want to hear.

I dip my fingers back into her trousers and pull her panties aside. This time, I push two fingers inside her, and she's soaking. Plunging my fingers in and out of Mila is better than sex. Her moans have me wanting her to come all over my fingers. I kiss her open mouth as she pants into mine. She's spreading her legs wider for me as I plunge another finger inside her.

"Oh, God!"

Her words are loud, and I move faster until she comes all over my fingers. Her tremors are delicious, and I don't slow down until she stops pushing herself down on my fingers.

I fix her panties back in place and remove my hand from her trousers. She's still clinging to my shoulders, and I don't move away. Inhaling deeply against her neck, I want to take her, but I don't want this to be the last time I'm inside her.

Mila drags my face to hers. Her gaze roams my face, and I could look at her for a long time; she's beautiful. I let her press a kiss to my lips. It's light to the touch, but it goes deeper than it should have. I feel the need to end this, like she's showing me how she feels and she's only doing it because there might not be a tomorrow. That thought terrifies me.

"I want you, Nicholai."

It's there for me to see. I can accept what I see in her eyes and give her what she wants. I smile softly. "You already have me, Mila."

I close the distance and kiss her deeply. There isn't anything soft about the kiss. It's edged with a panic I didn't sense coming over me and a savagery of wanting her now. She's quick to pull down her trousers, and I break the kiss to help her out of them. I'm tempted to move this inside, but she drags me back and I don't argue.

Her small hands work quickly at my belt, and the cold air on my ass has me pushing my body against her warmth. She easily spreads her legs, and I lift her up until my cock is right at her entrance. The contrast from the cold on my back to the heat of her against my flesh has me pushing into her soaking pussy. Its wetness and warmth consumes me, and I already feel my release building.

I'm moving quickly. My hands grip her thighs so I can hold her up and gain entry inside her. She's panting and pushing her body down on my cock, both of us pounding to the same rhythm. I'm aware of a car in the distance, but even if someone was standing behind me, I don't think I could stop fucking Mila. She's too good.

I move quicker, my hands digging into the flesh of her thighs. Her hands tighten around my neck as she moves with me faster. My release comes quickly, and I empty my seed inside her. She cries out along with me, and it's a new kind of ecstasy that I ride slowly back down.

Once our movements slow to a halt, I take a quick look around us. We haven't attracted attention. I turn back to Mila and place a soft kiss on her lips. Her eyes say too much. She's afraid and when she is with me, she should never feel that way. I slowly slip out of her, and silently, I help her back into her trousers before I pull up my own.

She deserves so much better than this piss-filled motel room, but I remind myself it will only be for a short while.

"I paid for a full week for the motel room," I tell her once we're inside. I don't look up at her as I take a few hundred out of my wallet and place it onto the table. "This is for food."

Silence makes me look up. Her eyes water with unshed tears. She surprises me when she nods. "When do you leave?"

"In the morning." I hope we make it to the morning without being caught. Once Oleg has me in the can, he'll call Gail off and that will keep Mila safe. She'll have no reason to keep hunting me.

"Okay." Mila drags the sleeves of her jumper down over her hands, her gaze darting away from me, and I'm ready to question her, but she picks up the remote and turns on the TV.

Tiredness pulls at me again, and I can't remember the last time I slept properly. I check the door and make sure it's locked before drawing the curtains. After pulling all the covers off the bed, I flip the stained mattress onto the other side. It doesn't look much better. I enter the bathroom and gather all the towels. I place them on the bed, then roll them out like a sheet.

"We should get some sleep."

Mila nods but doesn't look at me. "You go ahead. I just want to watch some TV."

"Mila." I say her name softly, and when she looks at me she smiles.

"I promise, I just need to settle my mind."

I walk over to her and press a kiss to her forehead. "Okay."

CHAPTER THIRTY TWO

MILA

There is one thing I'm certain of—that I won't let Nicholai go to the can for me. The only way I can try to do something about this is to go to Oleg. He's the one that wants me.

I'm tempted for the hundredth time to glance at Nicholai's sleeping form, but each time my heart races. What if he's still awake? Some documentary about an oil spill that's killing the seals plays out across the screen. It casts the room in flickers of light. Turning off the TV wouldn't be wise. There would be too much of a change in the room.

I count to ten before looking over my shoulder. His chest rises and falls in a steady rhythm. It's now or never. I get off the bed and walk toward the bathroom just to get a feel for how asleep he is. I keep an eye on Nicholai. I hadn't intended to go into the bathroom, but my feet seem to drag me that way. Once inside, I close my eyes and try to calm my racing heart. Going to Oleg is the only reasonable thing to do. I nod and open my eyes before leaving the bathroom. Nicholai is still asleep. I take a few bills off the table and leave the safety of the motel room.

It's cold tonight, but I try not to think about that. All I can think about is finding a taxi that will take me to Gail's. I remembered her home. It still feels bizarre that it was only today we were at her house, and that Nicholai had the photo of Gail, Dimitri, and Irina. My stomach churns thinking of Irina sitting on the swing.

Will Gail kill me? I highly doubt it, since Oleg wants me so badly, but she will have a direct line to him. I can't stop looking over my shoulder, expecting Nicholai to be there, but each time he isn't and I can't help the disappointment I feel at getting away. I know I'm doing the right thing, but that doesn't make it easy.

The town is close to the motel, and I don't have far to walk before I flag down a taxi. I climb in without an exact address, but I know the road.

"Farrah Street."

The driver doesn't start the car, and everything in me freezes. Have I made a mistake? His gray moustache and peaky cap make him look like so many other cabbies.

"Where exactly on Farrah Street?"

My heart slows down. I'm being paranoid. "I'll let you know."

The car starts up, and I glance out the window at all the people who walk down the street. They're oblivious to the freedom given to them. I don't think I have ever walked down a street without looking over my shoulder or without the thought in the back of my mind of someone wanting to harm me. I sink further into the seat and wish, for the millionth time, that I had been born into a normal life with a normal family.

The high wall along Farrah Street has me sitting forward. "Here is perfect."

The cab pulls in along the curb. I hand him a twenty and climb out. My stomach churns. I'm going to enter the woman's home whose child I helped kidnap. A shiver races down my spine. Folding my arms across my chest, I walk up the hill toward Gail's home.

A large hand clamps across my mouth, and my back collides with the wall painfully. I have no idea who I'm expecting, but it isn't Nicholai. His dark eyes swirl with anger.

"What are you doing?" His words come out in a hiss.

"Fixing this." I push him away from me but find myself pinned against the wall.

"How?" He's trying to calm himself, but it isn't working.

"By going to Gail's and getting her to ring Oleg."

There's a brief moment of silence before Nicholai pushes off the wall and releases me. He starts to laugh, and heat races up my neck.

"Are you that daft?" His words are snarled at me. I haven't ever seen this anger from Nicholai, and I don't like it.

"At least I'm not the one sending myself to the can. *That's* daft," I fire back, my own temper flaring. He can be allowed to do reckless things, and I'm not?

Nicholai moves and I'm boxed in again. "You kidnapped her child. She'll kill you on first glance."

"I'm worth more alive than dead." I really hope that much is true.

"You can't guarantee that, Mila." He pushes away from the wall again, and I have an overwhelming urge to touch him and try to calm him down.

I need to make him understand. I take a calming breath and move closer to him. He leans into my hand as I touch his face.

"I love you, Nicholai. I can't let you give yourself up for me." I adore the transformation I see in his eyes as my words fully register with him. It calms him and he moves his face and presses a kiss into my palm. Reaching up, he pulls my hand into his. My stomach flutters when I see the understanding in his eyes. He knows I'm doing the right thing. I'm ready to step toward him and give him a kiss when he starts walking in the opposite direction, bringing me with him.

"What are you doing?" I tug at my arm. He stops walking but doesn't let me go.

"Taking you back to the motel, where I'm going to have to hand-cuff you to the bed."

I point behind us, reminding him of the conversation we had like a second ago. "I thought you understood why I have to do it."

"I do understand, Mila. But I'm not letting you do it." He continues to walk, and no matter how much I pull at my hand to get it out of his, he won't loosen his hold on me.

"How the hell did you find me?" I finally ask when I can't break his hold on my hand.

"I placed a chip in your neck."

I drag my heels until he stops and faces me. "You're joking."

His dark gaze assesses my face. "No, Mila. I'm not." My stomach twists with the truth I see in his eyes.

I reach back and my fingers dance across the back of my neck. I move closer to the hairline and gasp. I feel a bump under my flesh.

"You put a chip in me?" I frown as a new sense of betrayal takes over.

"I don't regret it." Nicholai starts walking again, and I follow, giving up on getting out of his hold.

CHAPTER THIRTY THREE

NICHOLAI

I ALWAYS SEEM TO have that moment of regret after telling Mila something. She's fuming over the chip. We've been back in the motel room for the last ten minutes, and she keeps touching the back of her neck.

"I want it out." She slams a hand on her hip, her blue eyes on fire with anger.

"I will. I just can't right now."

She shakes her head. "How can I even trust a word you say?"

"You're talking to me about trust? You just ran off the moment I fell asleep."

She doesn't even look guilty. "I will run again. What I was doing was right."

Losing my temper isn't something that happens to me. Even when I exact revenge on someone, it's always done with a sense of calm, but right now, I can't seem to find anything calming about this situation.

"I won't hesitate to tie you up." I close the distance between us, and she doesn't shy away from me. She leans back.

"You put a chip in my neck." Her words are lower, but they sound more distraught now.

She doesn't understand. I exhale loudly and try to find my calm. "I love you," I say. Her shoulders grow rigid, and her eyes dart from left to right. Her mouth opens and closes, but nothing comes out.

"I'm trying to keep you safe," I add, sensing that I'm winning right now.

"I'm trying to keep you safe, too." She takes a step toward me and wraps her arms around my torso. She feels good in my arms.

"I need you to promise me you'll stay here." I press a kiss to the top of her head.

She doesn't answer me.

"Mila?"

It takes another few seconds before she looks up at me. "I promise."

I'm not sure if I believe her, but we only have a few more hours before I leave to go to the can. I would be lying if I said I wasn't worried about what's going to happen, but this is the only way to keep her safe.

"Let's try to get some sleep."

Mila nods and we lie down on the towel-covered bed. I drag her against my chest, and that's how we fall asleep.

I expect her to try to leave throughout the night, but she's still there the next morning. I don't want to wake her, so I place a kiss on her forehead and leave the motel room. It's warm as I start walking through the parking lot. I pick an old navy station wagon parked near the back of the motel. Using my elbow, I smash the passenger window and let myself in. No alarm goes off on the old model. After climbing across the seats, I unlock the driver's door before walking around and getting in. I pull out the wires and spark them a few times before the car starts.

I glance back at the motel one final time before leaving Mila behind. The drive to the can seems longer than usual, but once I pull up, I take out my phone and send a message to say that I have delivered Mila to the can.

I park the car a bit away from the can and walk the rest of the way. The gun in my waistband gives me a sense of security that I'm sure isn't real. The burnt ground beneath my feet has my stomach tightening as I cross it and walk to the can.

Opening the door, I step into the concrete box. It's stuffy from the heat. Pulling the door closed behind me, all I have to do is wait. I just won't wait inside. Stepping back out, I lock the can and make my way around the small building. When Oleg comes, I will only have seconds to surprise him. I remove my jacket and place it on the ground. I don't think anyone will be coming soon, so I get comfortable as I wait for the sound of a car.

Time passes and as the day continues, the heat grows more intense. I regret not leaving a phone with Mila. I'd like to talk to her. Pulling out my phone, I drag up the app and see her red dot, moving fast. She's in a car and traveling out of town. I'm standing, ready to leave and stop her from doing something stupid, when a car pulls up. I slowly remove my gun and stay close to the wall.

The car stops and someone gets out. I hear his whistle. He's relaxed, like he's finally cashing in. My blood boils. What would he do if Mila was inside?

The lock rattles, and I use that moment to appear beside him, my gun drawn and pointed at his head. "Hello, Oleg."

He pauses and slowly glances at me. His face tightens. "Nicholai, you want to tell me what this is about?"

He continues unlocking the can. I fire a shot into the ground beside him and he jumps back.

"Mila isn't in there," I confirm.

He nods, taking a step back.

"You will take me to Victor." I point the gun at his car. "Now."

He shakes his head. "I can't just take you to Victor. Mila is his daughter."

I want to empty the gun into his face when I think of the marks he left on Mila. "I don't think Victor would like to hear how you beat his daughter." For the first time, I see real fear cross Oleg's face. "Or how you killed a girl in front of her."

He snorts, but he's worried. The tightness around his eyes is giving away his concern.

"Or how you and Dimitri lied about where she was. I don't think Victor will be happy to hear his daughter never ran away."

Oleg spits to his left. "So, what do you want?"

I take a step closer. "I already told you, Oleg. Take me to Victor."

He stares at me, and I don't flinch. "He won't believe you."

"Who said that's the reason I want to see him?" I say and point at the car. "Start walking."

Oleg does, and I make him stop before climbing into the car. Patting him down, I remove the gun from his waistband.

"Don't move." I keep the gun pointed at him as I search the car. I find one more gun in the glove compartment.

"Get in." I climb into the passenger seat and Oleg gets in. He slams the door like he might be able to stop this.

"I can't just take you to Victor."

He roars when the gun impacts with the side of his face. "You *will* take me to Victor," I say. "Now drive the fucking car."

He starts it up and we leave the can. I don't check my phone until we're on the road for a few minutes. Mila is still moving. She's going in the opposite direction. What is she doing? She's too far out for it to be Gail's. I have no idea what she's up to.

"Did you kill the girl?" Oleg asks me while dabbing at his bleeding face.

"No. That's what you would have wanted, and then you would have had me killed. I know all about your little plan with Gail."

He's smart enough to keep driving and not open his mouth to me again. I have no idea where Victor lives, so I won't know what I'm up against until I'm face-to-face with the man himself. Until then, I won't know for sure if Oleg deceived me or not.

CHAPTER THIRTY FOUR

MILA

I HATE HOW MY legs shake as I press the button on the gate. I have no other options. This isn't the brightest decision I've ever made, but it seemed like the best one in this situation.

"Hello, kitten."

I force a smile at Anita's voice and glance back at the cab, waving him to go. I'm not leaving here until someone helps me.

"Can I speak with Lucca?" I try not to shuffle. I can't see Anita, but I'm picturing her smiling. I get radio silence before the gates slowly start to open. I walk through and up to the front door. Lucca opens it. He doesn't look surprised to see me as he drags the door fully open.

"What does he need?"

I step into the hallway and meet Anita's eye. She's in a sky blue tight-fitted dress that leaves nothing to the imagination. Her eyes smile at me, and I focus back on Lucca. Now that I'm here I need to make him help me.

"He's gone to see my father."

Lucca closes the door, and I try to shake off the feeling of being a trapped animal.

"He should have run." Lucca speaks before turning to me. "What do you want from me?"

All the friendliness is gone now.

"I just need you to make a quick phone call and I'll be gone."

Anita laughs and pushes off the doorframe. "She's not in the family for two minutes and she's looking for favors."

I know most people would start throwing the weight of their father's name around, but I don't want anything from my father. So I focus on Lucca.

"Anita, give us a minute." Maybe he remembers who I am.

"See you around, kitten." Anita strolls from the hallway, and I'm left with a very intimidating Lucca. His silver eyes never leave my face as he takes another step toward me.

"I don't know if you're very smart or very stupid."

I swallow. "Nicholai put himself in the can and is waiting for Oleg so he can force Oleg to take him to my father."

Lucca curses and runs his hands through his dark hair. "He should have run," he repeats.

"I need to get there and convince my father not to kill Nicholai." That's my grand plan.

"I'm sorry, but I don't exactly have a direct line to your father."

No one does. Not even me. My father doesn't like technology. He's paranoid, thinking someone is always listening in on him. That's why you have to go through his secretary, whose number I have no idea of.

"I need you to ring Eric."

Lucca raises both eyebrows. "Eric? Who Nicholai shot?"

I exhale loudly. I didn't think this would be easy, but I also don't need Lucca to make this harder than it already is.

"Please, if you just ring Eric, I'll be out of your hair."

He's staring at mem and I try not to squirm under Lucca's heavy gaze.

"Don't move." He points at the floor, and I nod quickly as he leaves me in the foyer. I can only hope he's gone to ring Eric—who I have no doubt will return for me—or he's going to kill me.

CHAPTER THIRTY FIVE

NICHOLAI

The large white house is somewhere I can imagine the leader of the Bratva living. I've spotted ten snipers on the rooftops. They aren't hidden. Their positions are visible for effect. I keep the barrel of my gun pointed at the back of Oleg's head and hope he is important enough to get me in front of Victor.

"You're making a mistake." Oleg tries to turn around, but I push him forward.

"Keep walking." We climb five large marble steps and head into a sitting area that's empty.

"Where is he?" I want to shake Oleg, but I also don't want to take the gun from the back of his head.

"You know, if he wanted you dead, you'd be dead." I hate the gleam of pleasure in Oleg's gaze at this knowledge.

He keeps walking and we step out into a foyer. A long white pavement runs a few meters to a small sitting area, where under a large umbrella, a man sits, watching us.

"You should let me go," Oleg says, but I keep pushing us forward.

I spot more snipers out here, along with armed men along the house. None of them move, and the closer I get to Victor, I know I am alive at his grace. I'm just not sure how long that grace will be extended.

"Oleg, you brought The Collector to my home?" Victor's gray hair is slicked back from his tanned face. He picks up a large glass of red wine and drinks deeply, at ease as if his home hasn't just been invaded by an armed man.

"I didn't have much of a choice, boss." Oleg speaks up.

"We always have a choice, Oleg."

Victor's blue eyes spring to me, and I see Mila in his features. "I want you to throw your gun down. My men can take you out in a second. The only reason you're still breathing is because I'm very curious as to why The Collector has a gun pointed at my right-hand man's head."

I'm weighing my options while glancing around. I could be dead in a second either way. I had to give Victor something back, since he's the only reason I'm alive. I remove the gun from Oleg's head and put on the safety before throwing it on the grass alongside the white pavement.

Oleg steps away from me immediately. "Kill him," he commands.

Victor takes another drink and watches me over the rim. Once the glass is put down on the round table, he speaks. "Be quiet, Oleg."

Now Victor's attention is on me.

"I have your daughter," I start with. He doesn't seem surprised at all. "Oleg and Dimitri lied to you. She never ran away. They hid her."

Oleg starts to laugh.

For the first time, I see a flicker of anger in Victor's gaze as he cuts across to Oleg. "I know what he has done. I know how he deceived me all those years ago."

I hadn't expected him to know.

"I didn't..." Oleg starts, and Victor holds up a finger.

"You hid my daughter from me because she took my attention away from the business with all her antics." He circles his hand in the air. "I understand why you did it, and I allowed it to go ahead because I agreed, but don't stand here and lie to me."

This isn't going the way I expected at all. He knew what Oleg and Dimitri had done to his daughter.

Now Victor turns back to me. "Is that why you brought Oleg here? To confess his sins? Tell me, Nicholai, what are your sins?"

"He tried to kill her and me," I fire out.

"He's lying." Oleg speaks out of turn again, and I see the warning in Victor's gaze.

Oleg falls silent and Victor returns his heavy gaze to me. "You have proof?" Victor asks.

"No, only your daughter's word."

Victor glances behind me. "Where is she?"

I can tell from the look in his eyes that he already knows that Mila isn't here.

"She's safe." I glance at Oleg. "He murdered a girl in front of Mila."

Surprise filters through Victor's gaze, and I pray this is a turn in the right direction.

Oleg narrows his gaze at me before turning back to Victor. He seems to weigh his words. "It was a whore. She got out of hand and things got intense."

Victor nods. "Mila witnessed this?"

Oleg's face has paled. "Boss, I didn't..."

Victor smiles and stands up. His fingers are coated in rings he joins together. He walks to Oleg and places a hand on his left shoulder. "You have been loyal to me since you were a boy."

Oleg nods, but worry starts to fill his eyes.

"That's why I made you my right-hand man. You hid my daughter away, and I allowed it because the intent was good. So now old friend, tell me. Did you try to have her killed?"

Oleg shakes his head. He is hardly going to admit trying to kill Mila. It's an instant death sentence. "No, boss. He's lying."

Victor squeezes Oleg's shoulder again and nods. "Okay, Oleg."

He steps away from Oleg and walks back to his seat. It's the smallest of movements, but he raises his index finger. The whoosh of a bullet has me spinning as it impales itself in the back of Oleg's head. He hits the ground just as Victor sits back down. He doesn't glance at Oleg's body but picks up his glass of wine and takes a sip. My gaze is assessing his fingers, watching for him to raise one.

"Do you think it was wise to come to my home?"

"No, but I had to keep Mila safe. I knew you were the only person capable of doing that."

Victor stares at me. I want to remove my tie and jacket, as the heat of the sun and this situation has sweat slowly making a pathway down my back.

"What do you think will happen when word gets out that The Collector entered my home with my right-hand man at gunpoint?"

"I'm sure everyone will know I only entered at your grace. You could have had me killed at the gate." I'm aware the gun is only four large strides to my left. I wouldn't have much of a chance of getting out of here, but if I had Victor at gunpoint, I might be able to stay alive until I got far enough away I could get Mila and run.

He picks up the glass again, and I notice his pinky finger raises ever so slightly. I dive as a bullet is released from a sniper on the roof. The impact tears through my side as I slam into the ground.

CHAPTER THIRTY SIX

MILA

Eric doesn't speak the whole drive. I insisted on driving since he can only use one leg, but his car has automatic transmission. He looks far too pale to be driving, but he wouldn't give in. I knew he would come when Lucca rang him. I just wasn't so sure he would take me to my father.

We pull up at my father's home. Once they see Eric driving, they let us pass. I don't say anything as I climb out of the car. My stomach is in knots. Please God, tell me I'm not too late. I enter the house and am very aware of the amount of armed men. I move quickly through the sitting room. My home the last six years would fit into the hall four times over.

"Maybe we should let your father know we're here before you go out there."

I ignore Eric and step out into the foyer. The blood in my veins freezes. Two bodies are on the white pavement, both pooling with blood. I sense my father's heavy gaze on me as I run toward Nicholai.

"Nicholai!" I pull him around, and he groans out in pain.

"Mila, what are you doing here?" His words are breathy.

I smile with relief that he isn't dead, but he is losing a lot of blood. I press down on the wound along his side, and for the first time, look up at my father, who watches me over the rim of a wineglass.

"Hello, Mila."

I want to spit at him. "Let me take him to a hospital."

My father smiles. There's nothing fatherly or warm about his smile.

"Why?" he asks, and I glance back down at Nicholai, whose skin seems to pale further.

"Please, Father! I'll do anything!" I plead.

"Anything?" My father takes a drink, like the blood flowing from Nicholai isn't alarming.

"Yes, anything!" I shout.

Laughter bubbles up from my father's mouth. "Very well, Mila. Pick up the gun to your left." I glance over to where my father indicates and see a gun. My stomach churns as I glance back at him.

"Shoot The Collector and then you can take him to a hospital."

"What?" Warm liquid flows over my fingers.

"Shoot him and then you can take him to a hospital. Prove your loyalty to me."

Nicholai's breathing is growing more faint. I know I'm running out of time.

"You've always hated me." A lump in my throat nearly chokes me. "I'm your only child, and I'm begging you to let me take care of the man I love."

Tears spill and I hate the man I'm looking up at. There is no remorse in his face.

He takes a large drink. "The decision is yours, Mila."

I'm up and race to the gun. My blood-soaked fingers wrap around it, and I point the gun at my father. "I should kill you!"

His laughter has my hand shaking. "Don't be foolish. Look around you, Mila. I raise one finger and you die. I think we both know I won't hesitate, so either shoot The Collector or watch him die at your feet."

I hate him. I have no other emotion, only hate for this man. I lower the gun because I know I can't win with anger. I slowly step back over to Nicholai. He blinks and looks up at me as I point the gun at him.

"Just do it." His words are low, but I hate them. I swallow the saliva that pools in my mouth, along with the tears that refuse to stop falling.

"What if it kills you?" My hand shakes.

"If you don't shoot me, I'm going to die here, Mila. Aim for my shoulder, try not to hit... any organs."

He's smiling with his eyes closed like this is a joke.

"I'm waiting." My father sounds very pleased with himself.

I glance back at Nicholai. "I love you," I tell him before I pull the trigger.

EPILOGUE

MILA

There are times when the decisions we make shape us to become better people. We grow from our circumstances. We grow from good and bad decisions. We grow in general. I think since meeting Nicholai, that's exactly what's happened to me. I've grown so much. I've lost a lot and gained even more.

I glance over my shoulder and smile at Nicholai as he walks toward me with two beers. We've parked up on the Rocky Mountains and are watching as the sun starts to set. I take the cold beer as Nicholai joins me on the hood of the car.

It's been three months since I shot him. My gaze travels to his shoulder, which always seems stiff. I hate myself for hurting him, but it was also the only way to save him from my father, who I swore I would never speak to again. I honestly don't think my father cares if he sees me or not, and I haven't spoken to Nicholai about it. I don't want to talk about that day.

I lean into Nicholai, and he circles his arm around my shoulder. I love the smell of him as he leans in close and plants a kiss on my head.

"Are you happy?" he asks. It's something he asks me a lot. Maybe I look sad when I start to think, but with time, I know that will ease. I have my family right beside me, and that's all that matters.

"When I'm with you, I am." I smile up into his handsome face and love how his dark eyes drink me up before he bows down and places a kiss on my lips.

"Did I tell you how lucky I am?"

I laugh at his question. "Every day." And he does.

He takes a deep swallow from his bottle while his phone bleeps, and I hate the sound it makes. He takes it out and reads it.

"Is it a collection?" I ask, hating that he still has to work for my father. A part of me feels I should stay in contact with my dad so I can get Nicholai out of the Bratva, but I'm not ready to face that demon yet.

"It doesn't matter. All that matters is that you're here, in my arms." He tightens an arm around me.

"I wish you didn't have to do it anymore." The words are useless.

"No one leaves, Mila."

I frown up at him, reaching up to touch his face. "Maybe you can be the exception to that rule." Pain tightens around my throat when his dark eyes grow sad.

"Maybe." He leans in and presses a kiss to my forehead.

"I hate him," I tell the setting sun. I don't have to explain to Nicholai who I'm talking about. He knows.

"Do you want to know why he killed Oleg?"

My stomach churns, and I take a deep drink from the bottle. "Why?"

"Because he put his hands on you."

My head snaps up to Nicholai. I'm looking for deceit in his words, and I hold out hope that maybe, just maybe, my father cares. It makes me feel foolish that I could for one second hope.

"I know he hasn't done right by you, but you are still his daughter."

I'm ready to look away when Nicholai stops me by placing his fingers under my chin. "I know right now it's too hard, but in time, you should try to forgive him."

I snort. "He made me shoot you," I remind him.

He smiles like he admires my father for that. "I'm here," Nicholai says.

I don't want an argument, and especially not about my father.

"Yeah, I'll think about it," I say. Maybe one day I can become strong enough to speak to him about letting Nicholai go. That will be the only conversation I would ever have with my father.

Nicholai pulls me into his side. "I'm so lucky that I found you."

I relax into his touch. "I suppose you are," I tease, and smile up at him.

His gaze skims my face before he presses his lips against mine. Just like every other single time, my whole body comes alive with a want for Nicholai that I don't believe will ever be quenched.

THE HANDLER: BOOK TWO IS OUT NOW. WANT TO READ ABOUT LUCCA?

Start Reading Today!

THE HANDLER #2 / The Cells of Kalashov Series / Books | authorvicarter